T.V. MANIA!

T.V. fans, once again it's time to broadcast your talents with this all-new line-up of terrific T.V. teasers!

First, tune in your trivia air waves with this tantalizing sample:

— In *Star Trek*: What was the color of Mr. Spock's blood?
— In *The Rockford Files*: How much did Jim Rockford charge per day for his services?
— In *Dark Shadows*: What was the name of the haunted mansion?
— In *Mission: Impossible*: How many seconds did it take for the tape to self-destruct?
— In *The Beverly Hillbillies*: What town did the Clampetts live in before their move to Beverly Hills?
— In *The Mary Tyler Moore Show*: What was the name of Sue Ann Niven's television program?
— In *Happy Days*: What was the Fonzie's nickname for Mrs. Cunningham?
— In *That Girl*: What was Ann Marie's career?
— In *I Love Lucy*: Who played Fred Mertz?
— In *Petticoat Junction*: Which one of the Bradley girls married Steve Elliott?

For answers to these and more than a thousand others, keep on reading. Surrender yourself to T.V. mania and become the trivia hit of the season!

TRIVIA MANIA
by Xavier Einstein

TRIVIA MANIA has arrived! With enough questions to answer every trivia buff's dreams, TRIVIA MANIA covers it all—from the delightfully obscure to the seemingly obvious. Tickle your fancy, and test your memory!

TELEVISION VOLUME II

TRIVIA Mania

BY XAVIER EINSTEIN

ZEBRA BOOKS
KENSINGTON PUBLISHING CORP.

The author would like to thank Gary Mercer and Ricky and Lee Taub for their assistance in the preparation of this book.

ZEBRA BOOKS

are published by

Kensington Publishing Corp.
475 Park Avenue South
New York, N.Y. 10016

First printing: August, 1984

Printed in the United States of America

TRIVIA MANIA:
Television (Vol. II)

1) Who was Mr. Spock's first captain in the science fiction series *Star Trek*?

2) What was the code name of Starsky and Hutch's squad car in the police series with the same name?
   a. Zebra 3
   b. Tiger 3
   c. Eagle 3
   d. Leopard 3

3) Before he became a private detective, Jim Rockford had been in prison in the series *The Rockford Files*. True or False?

4) What was the name of Ben Cartwright's horse in the western *Bonanza*?

5) What was the name of the millionaire's wife in the sitcom *Gilligan's Island*?

6) Who was Darrin Stevens's boss in the sitcom *Bewitched*?

7) Who was the commanding officer of the S.W.A.T. squad in the police series *S.W.A.T.*?

. . . Answers

1. Captain Christopher Pike

2. a

3. True

4. Buck

5. Mrs. Lovey Howell III

6. Larry Tate

7. Captain Harrelson

8) What was the name of the ranch on which the western *Empire* was based?

9) Who were the producers of the *Jonny Quest* cartoon series?

10) What was the monetary value of the bill that each of the Maverick brothers had pinned inside his coat in the western *Maverick*?
   a. $50
   b. $100
   c. $1000
   d. none of these

11) Greenpoint was the name of the town in which the gang lived in the *Our Gang* series, also known as *The Little Rascals*. True or False?

12) Dwayne Hickman (Dobie Gillis) was most incompatible with this actress who portrayed Thalia Menninger in the sitcom *The Many Loves of Dobie Gillis*.

13) Who were the four comedians in the comedy series *Four Star Revue*?

14) What was the name of Margie's father in the sitcom *My Little Margie*?

15) What was the name of Israel Boone's pet goose in the western *Daniel Boone*?

16) Who was Allison MacKenzie's real father in the soap *Peyton Place*?

17) In the sitcom *Ozzie's Girls*, what were the names of the two girls whom the Nelsons boarded?

. . . Answers

8. Garret

9. William Hanna and Joseph Barbera

10. c

11. True

12. Tuesday Weld

13. Ed Wynn, Danny Thomas, Jack Carson, and Jimmy Durante

14. Vernon Albright

15. Hannibal

16. Elliott Carson

17. Susie Hamilton and Brenda MacKenzie

18) Oswald Chesterfield Cobblepot was better known as which of the following villains in the *Batman* series:
   a. Riddler
   b. Joker
   c. Egghead
   d. Penguin

19) What actor portrayed Jim Bronson in the adventure series *Then Came Bronson*?

20) Who portrayed Cameron in the adventure series *Search*?

21) What character did Chuck Conners portray in the western *Branded*?

22) Who portrayed Sheena in *Sheena, Queen of the Jungle*?

23) What character did Ken Osmond portray in the sitcom *Leave it to Beaver*?

24) Linc Case was a veteran of which war in the adventure series *Route 66*?
   a. World War II
   b. Korean
   c. Vietnam
   d. he was not a veteran of any war

25) What was the name of the Rileys' dog in the sitcom *The Life of Riley*?

26) What is the color of Mr. Spock's blood in the science fiction series *Star Trek*?
   a. purple
   b. red
   c. green
   d. brown

. . . Answers

18. d

19. Michael Parks

20. Burgess Meredith

21. Jason McCord

22. Irish McCalla

23. Eddie Haskell

24. c

25. Rex

26. c

27) The theme song for the "Freddie the Freeloader" skits on the *Red Skelton Show* was "Huggable Clown." True or False?

28) What hard-drinking Englishwoman replaced Florida Evans as Maude's second maid in the sitcom *Maude*?

29) Who played the part of Alec Fleming in the comedy series *The Rogues*?

30) From what show are these words: "You heard it from the horse's mouth"?

31) Grindl in the sitcom of the same name worked for Foster's Temporary Employment Service. True or False?

32) What was the name of Zorro's deaf servant in the western *Zorro*?

33) How many children did Carolyn Muir have in the sitcom *The Ghost and Mrs. Muir*?

34) Dr. Tom Reynolds was the son of missionaries in the adventure series *Ramar of the Jungle*. True or False?

35) What was the name of the one-toothed dragon in the children's series *Kukla, Fran, & Ollie*?

36) Who was Sheriff Lobo's idiotic brother-in-law in the *Lobo* police comedy?

37) What character in a sitcom of the early 1960's liked the phrase "Ooh! Ooh! Ooh!"?

38) Who was the army psychiatrist who made occasional visits to the M.A.S.H. unit to evaluate their mental condition in the sitcom *M*A*S*H*?

. . . Answers

27. False, "Lovable Clown"

28. Mrs. Nell Naugatuck

29. David Niven

30. *Mr. Ed*

31. True

32. Bernardo

33. Two

34. True

35. Ollie or Oliver J. Dragon

36. Deputy Perkins

37. Gunther Toody, *Car 54, Where Are You?*

38. Dr. Sidney Freedman

39) Who was Mr. Waverly's secretary in the spy series *The Man from U.N.C.L.E.*?

40) What member of the Mod Squad was thrown out of his Beverly Hills home in the police series *The Mod Squad*?

41) What was the name of the Walton's hounddog in the drama series *The Waltons*?

42) What was the telephone number of Ralph and Alice Kramden in *The Honeymooners*?

43) What sitcom, telecast as the 1956 summer replacement for *I Love Lucy*, starred Charlie Farrell in the semi-autobiographical role of a host to vacationing Hollywooders?

44) What musical variety show featured the hit song "Tie a Yellow Ribbon 'Round the Old Oak Tree"?

45) On which local station did the *Fernwood 2-Night* talk show appear?
   a. WWAW-TV
   b. WXAX-TV
   c. WZAZ-TV
   d. WYAY-TV

46) Stretch Cunningham was a character in what famous sitcom?

47) The One-Armed Man was captured and sent to prison at the conclusion of *The Fugitive*. True or False?

48) Was Bronco Layne of the western *Bronco* an ex-Confederate or ex-Yankee Army captain?

49) What type of pistol did Emma Peel of the spy series *The Avengers* use?

. . . *Answers*

39. Lisa Rogers

40. Pete Cochran

41. Reckless

42. BEnsonhurst 0-7741

43. *The Charlie Farrell Show*

44. *Tony Orlando and Dawn*

45. c

46. *All in the Family*

47. False, he was killed

48. Ex-Confederate

49. Italian Beretta 7.65 pistol

QUESTIONS

50) In what city was Chief Petty Officer Sharkey of the U.S. Navy stationed in the sitcom *C.P.O. Sharkey*?
   a. San Jose
   b. San Diego
   c. San Francisco
   d. San Bernardino

51) *The Defenders* had its origin in a story written by what author?

52) What were the names of Laverne & Shirley's truck-driving neighbors in the sitcom *Laverne & Shirley*?

53) Who was the stringent corrections officer in the sitcom *On the Rocks*?

54) What was the name of Barnaby Jones's young cousin who joined his investigative firm in the detective series *Barnaby Jones*?

55) Harry Grafton was a civilian in the sitcom *The New Phil Silvers Show*. True or False?

56) "I Walk the Line" was the closing theme song of what musical variety show which was first telecast in the summer of 1969?

57) What was the name of Arnie Nuvo's former blue collar co-worker with whom he had remained in contact in the sitcom *Arnie*?

58) What character in the *Abbott and Costello Show* was known for the line "I'll harm you!"?

59) What character did Paul Lynde portray in the sitcom *The Paul Lynde Show*?

... *Answers*

50. b

51. Reginald Rose

52. Lenny and Squiggy

53. Mr. Gibson

54. Jedediah Romano Jones or J. R.

55. True

56. *The Johnny Cash Show*

57. Julius

58. Stinky

59. Paul Simms

60) Who was the hostess of a musical variety show whose theme song was "See the U.S.A. in your Chevrolet"?

61) What was the name of the main street in the soap opera *Peyton Place*?

62) What was Keith Anderson also known as in the sitcom *Good Times*?

63) What was the name of the hotel where Jose Jimenez worked as a bellhop in the sitcom *The Bill Dana Show*?
   a. Golden Galley Hotel
   b. Regal Ritz Hotel
   c. Park Central Hotel
   d. Silver Star Hotel

64) What were the first names of the two Grainger brothers who at one time owned the Shiloh Ranch in the western *The Virginian*?

65) Who was the owner of Howard Publications in the adventure series *The Name of the Game*?

66) Beau McCloud was Jim Hardie's assistant in the western *Tales of Wells Fargo*. True or False?

67) What were the names of the two children in the sitcom *The Addams Family*?

68) What actor portrayed Hopalong Cassidy in the western of the same name?

69) From what suspense series was the following quote taken: "Sunrise and sunset, promise and fulfillment, birth and death — the whole drama of life is written in the Sands of Time"?

. . . *Answers*

60. Dinah Shore, *The Dinah Shore Chevy Show*

61. Elm Street

62. Kool Aid

63. c

64. John and Clay

65. Glenn Howard

66. True

67. Pugsley and Wednesday

68. William Boyd

69. *The Clock*

QUESTIONS

70) How much money did Ricky Ricardo earn per week at the Tropicana Club in the *I Love Lucy* shows?
- a. $150
- b. $200
- c. $250
- d. $300

71) What western star had introduced the first TV episode of *Gunsmoke*?

72) Who was the Latin elevator operator in the sitcom *Make Room for Daddy*?

73) Who was Stewart and Sally MacMillan's maid in the police series *MacMillan and Wife*?

74) To what TV series does the following license number belong: C12563?

75) What was the name of Shad and Gronk's son who was saved by the two astronauts in the sitcom *It's About Time*?

76) What relation was Pearl Bodine to Jethro in the sitcom *The Beverly Hillbillies*?
- a. mother
- b. aunt
- c. grandmother
- d. cousin

77) How many shots were fired from Lucas McCain's rifle in the opening of *The Rifleman* series?

78) In the underwater adventure series *Sea Hunt*, who played Mike Nelson?

79) What was the sitcom *The Jeannie Carson Show* originally titled?

. . . Answers

70. a

71. John Wayne

72. Jose Jimenez

73. Mildred

74. *Ironside*, number of Robert Ironside's wagon

75. Breer

76. a

77. 11

78. Lloyd Bridges

79. *Hey Jeannie*

QUESTIONS

80) What did the Flintstones name their daughter in the cartoon series *The Flintstones*?

81) What was the name of Pinky Tuscadero's sister in the sitcom *Happy Days*?

82) In what hotel was Cricket Blake a singer in the detective series *Hawaiian Eye*?

83) What company sponsored *The $64,000 Question*?

84) What was the name of Cameron Brooks's hometown in the sitcom *Window on Main Street*?

85) How much did Jim Rockford charge per day for his services in the detective series *The Rockford Files*?

86) Who was the only left-handed member of the Cartwright family in the western series *Bonanza*?

87) Who was the "Chief's" superior in the sitcom *Get Smart*?

88) What was the name of Nick Barkley's horse in the western *The Big Valley*?

89) What was Captain Harrelson's nickname in the police series *S.W.A.T.*?

90) What was the name of the ranch foreman in the western *Empire*?

91) What did Master Po call Caine in the *Kung Fu* series?
   a. Beaver
   b. Grasshopper
   c. Hawk
   d. Firefly

... *Answers*

80. Pebbles

81. Leather Tuscadero

82. Hawaiian Village Hotel

83. Revlon

84. Millsburg

85. $200 plus expenses

86. Joe

87. Zebra 642

88. Coco

89. "Hondo"

90. Jim Redigo

91. b

92) Monday was "Guest Star Day" on the *Mickey Mouse Club* series. True or False?

93) What famous phrase did Tonto say to the Lone Ranger which means "faithful friend" in the western *The Lone Ranger*?

94) What was the name of the army base were Dobie Gillis and Maynard G. Krebs were sent for basic training in *The Many Loves of Dobie Gillis*?

95) Who starred in a mind reading series which was released in 1971 and contained 90 episodes?

96) Irma Peterson was a maid in the sitcom *My Friend Irma*. True or False?

97) What was the name of the haunted mansion in the *Dark Shadows* series?

98) Who was Rodney Harrington's lawyer during his murder trial in the soap *Peyton Place*?

99) What actor portrayed "Thorny" Thornberry in the sitcom *The Adventures of Ozzie & Harriet*?

100) What enemy of Batman did Julie Newmar, Eartha Kitt, and Lee Meriwether portray in the adventure series *Batman*?

101) What was the name of the Curtis family's barbershop in the sitcom *That's My Mama*?
   a. Junior's
   b. Oscar's
   c. Earl's
   d. Josh's

102) What character did Tony Franciosa play in the adventure series *Search*?

. . . Answers

92. False, Monday was "Fun With Music Day"

93. "Kemo sabe"

94. Camp Grace

95. Kreskin, *The Amazing World of Kreskin*

96. False, a secretary

97. Collinwood

98. Steven Cord

99. Don DeFore

100. Catwoman

101. b

102. Nick Bianco

103) Who were the father and son cops featured in the police series *Brenner*?

104) What country was the setting for *Sheena, Queen of the Jungle*?

105) Who was Beaver's rotund friend who was always eating in the sitcom *Leave it to Beaver*?

106) Who was the officer best known for his marksmanship in the police drama *S.W.A.T.*?

107) Who was the town drunk in the sitcom *The Andy Griffith Show*?

108) On what deck were the sleeping quarters of Captain Kirk in the science fiction series *Star Trek*?

109) What was the name of the boxer characterized by Red Skelton on *The Red Skelton Show*?

110) Who did Dr. Arthur Harmon marry in the sitcom *Maude*?

111) Who were the two families featured in the comedy series *The Rogues*?

112) What was the name of Mr. Magoo's dog?

113) What was the name of the conniving Indian in the sitcom *Guestwood Ho*?

114) Phantom was the name of Zorro's black horse in the western *Zorro*. True or False?

115) Which one of Carolyn Muir's children slept in the ghost's bedroom in the sitcom *The Ghost and Mrs. Muir*?

. . . *Answers*

103. Det. Lt. Roy Brenner and son Ernie Brenner

104. Kenya

105. Larry Mondello

106. Officer Dominic Luca

107. Otis Campbell

108. Deck 5

109. Cauliflower McPugg

110. Vivian Cavender

111. Flemings and St. Clairs

112. Bowser

113. Hawkeye

114. False, Tornado

115. Candy

QUESTIONS

116) What was the name of the professor portrayed by Ray Montgomery in the adventure series *Ramar of the Jungle*?

117) George Amadio was Carl Kolchak's editor in the occult series *Kolchak: The Night Stalker*. True or False?

118) Who was Deputy Birdie Hawkins's girlfriend in the *Lobo* police comedy?

119) What would Gunther Toody say to those who got in his way in the sitcom *Car 54, Where Are You*?

120) Who did Col. Sherman Potter replace in the sitcom *M*A*S*H*?

121) What lieutenant was Joe Mannix's friend and police contact in the detective series *Mannix*?

122) Who was Mork's boss in the sitcom *Mork & Mindy*?

123) In the *Wonder Woman* adventure series, what relation is Queen Hippolyte to Wonder Woman?
    a. grandmother
    b. mother
    c. sister
    d. aunt

124) What was the name of the Indian princess in the children's series *Howdy Doody Time*?

125) Who was the last of the original three angels to be cast in the detective series *Charlie's Angels*?

126) Who was the Court of Common Pleas Judge in the sitcom *The Tony Randall Show*?

. . . *Answers*

116. Professor Ogden

117. False, Tony Vincenzo

118. Sarah Cumberland

119. "Do you mind? Do-you-Mind!?"

120. Lt. Col. Henry Blake

121. Lt. Adam Tobias

122. Orson

123. b

124. Princess Summerfall-Winterspring

125. Farrah Fawcett-Majors

126. Judge Walter Franklin

127) What sitcom of the early 1960's was based on a Minnesota farm girl's new life in a congressman's home in Washington, D.C.?

128) What was Archie's nickname for Michael Stivic in the sitcom *All in the Family*?

129) Garrison's Gorillas of the war series with the same name had their headquarters in France. True or False?

130) What was "The Captain's" real name in the musical variety show *The Captain & Tennille*?

131) What TV character prefers his tea with three lumps of sugar stirred counterclockwise?

132) What actor portrayed C.P.O. Sharkey in the sitcom with the same name?

133) What was the badge number of Sgt. Joe Friday in the series *Dragnet*?
  a. 712
  b. 714
  c. 716
  d. 718

134) Who was known as "The Big Ragu" in the sitcom *Laverne & Shirley*?

135) *"Sea Serpent"* was the name of the featured submarine in the sitcom *Operation Petticoat*. True or False?

136) What character in the sitcom *Barney Miller* was continually attracted to the prostitutes that he arrested?

137) Who emceed *The Newlywed Game*?

. . . *Answers*

127. *The Farmer's Daughter*

128. Meathead

129. False, England

130. Daryl Dragon

131. John Steed, *The Avengers*

132. Don Rickles

133. b

134. Carmine Ragusa

135. False, *Sea Tiger*

136. Detective Wojohowicz

137. Bob Eubanks

QUESTIONS

138) Hadji was Jonny Quest's young Indian friend in the cartoon series *Jonny Quest*. True or False?

139) What was the name of the crime series which starred Ben Gazzara as Det. Sgt. Nick Anderson?

140) What character did Gordon Jones portray in *The Abbott and Costello Show*?

141) What character did Frances Rafferty portray in the sitcom *Pete and Gladys*?
    a. Heather
    b. Kimber
    c. Nancy
    d. Valerie

142) Shelley Fabares, who portrayed Mary Stone in the sitcom *The Donna Reed Show*, had a 1962 hit single called "Johnny Angel." True or False?

143) Who was Sweet Pea's pet in the *Popeye* cartoons?

144) What character did Bernadette Stanis portray in the sitcom *Good Times*?

145) What was the name of Bing Collins's wife in the sitcom *The Bing Crosby Show*?

146) Judge Henry Garth was the first owner of the Shiloh Ranch in the western *The Virginian*. True or False?

147) Which of the following actors did not star in the adventure series *The Name of the Game*?
    a. James Franciscus
    b. Gene Barry
    c. Robert Stack
    d. Tony Franciosa

. . . Answers

138. True

139. *Arrest and Trial*

140. Mike the Cop

141. c

142. True

143. Eugene the Jeep

144. Thelma Evans Anderson

145. Ellie Collins

146. True

147. a

148) What were the names of Widow Ovie's two daughters in the western *Tales of Wells Fargo*?

149) What was the name of the uncle in the sitcom *The Addams Family*?

150) What actress portrayed Loco Jones in the sitcom *How to Marry a Millionaire*?

151) What music series, first telecast in the spring of 1953, featured a fifteen-minute show with an idol of the bobbysoxers?

152) What was the name of the judge of the sitcom *I Married Joan*?

153) What was the name of the street in Dodge City where the Long Branch Saloon was located in the western *Gunsmoke*?

154) What actress portrayed Mrs. Margaret Williams in the sitcom *The Danny Thomas Show*?

155) How many seconds would pass before the tape would self-destruct in the intrigue series *Mission: Impossible*?
   a. five
   b. six
   c. seven
   d. nine

156) What was the name of the prison in which Alexander Mundy served time in *It Takes a Thief*?

157) Who was the nonconformist surgeon in the sitcom *House Calls*?

158) Who was the bird-watching friend of Bob Collins in *Love That Bob* who was later cast in *The Beverly Hillbillies*?

... Answers

148. Mary Gee and Tina

149. Uncle Fester

150. Barbara Eden

151. *Coke Time with Eddie Fisher*

152. Judge Bradley Stevens

153. Front Street

154. Jean Hagen

155. a

156. San Jobal Prison

157. Dr. Charley Michaels

158. Nancy Kulp as Pamela Livingston and later Jane Hathaway

159) What was the name of Mark McCain's horse in *The Rifleman*?

160) Marineland of the Pacific was the museum which employed Mike Nelson in the adventure series *Sea Hunt*. True or False?

161) What actress portrayed Woody's sister in the sitcom *Hey Landlord*?
    a. Pamela Rodgers
    b. Ann Morgan Guilbert
    c. Sally Field
    d. Angela Cartwright

162) What cartoon characters live at 345 Stone Cave Road?

163) Who was Stella's main adversary in the sitcom *Harper Valley P.T.A.*?

164) What was the name of the palace which served as the seat of the Hawaiian government in *Hawaii Five-O*?

165) Who played James Slattery in the political drama *Slattery's People*?

166) Who were the three reporters featured in the newspaper series *Wire Service*?

167) Who was Jim Rockford's romantic interest in the detective series *The Rockford Files*?

168) The following TV wives were at different times married to what TV husband: Elizabeth, Inger, and Marie?

169) What was "Big Tom" in the sitcom *The Good Guys*?
    a. taxi driver   c. truck driver
    b. dishwasher   d. policeman

. . . Answers

159. Blue Boy

160. True

161. c

162. Barney and Betty Rubble, *The Flintstones*

163. Flora Simpson Reilly

164. Iolani Palace

165. Richard Crenna

166. Dan Miller, Dean Evans, and Katherine Wells

167. Beth Davenport

168. Ben Cartwright, *Bonanza*

169. c

170) Samantha's warlock Uncle Arthur was portrayed by what actor in the sitcom *Bewitched*?

171) A stick figure with a halo was depicted on a calling card in what mystery adventure series?

172) The "squawk box" was a frequent expression of the sailors in this sitcom of the early 1960's.

173) Who was the "lawman" in the western with the same name?

174) The Millionaire's estate was known as Silverstone in the series *The Millionaire*. True or False?

175) What was the name of Bob Collins's widowed sister in the comedy series *Love That Bob*?

176) What was the name of the statue which was shown with Dobie Gillis at the beginning and end of each episode in *The Many Loves of Dobie Gillis*?

177) Who was known as the "big dummy" in the sitcom *Amos 'N' Andy*?

178) What actress portrayed Margie Albright in the sitcom *My Little Margie*?

179) "Whipped Cream" was the theme song of what game show?

180) What *Peyton Place* character was married to Rodney Harrington twice and Steven Cord once?

... *Answers*

170. Paul Lynde

171. *The Saint*

172. *Ensign O'Toole*

173. Marshal Dan Troop

174. True

175. Margaret MacDonald

176. *The Thinker*

177. Andy Brown

178. Gale Storm

179. *The Dating Game*

180. Betty Anderson

181) Who was Robin Hood's girlfriend in *The Adventures of Robin Hood*?
   a. Maid Matilda
   b. Maid Marie
   c. Maid Marian
   d. Maid Maureen

182) Name a famous duo portrayed by Adam West and Burt Ward in this television fantasy adventure.

183) What was Beatrice Dane's alias in the comedy series *The Thin Man*?

184) Where did Edwin Carpenter live in the sitcom *The Second Hundred Years*?

185) What was *The Brian Keith Show* formerly called?

186) What was the name of Sheena's chimpanzee in the adventure series *Sheena, Queen of the Jungle*?

187) At what camp was Lt. William Rice stationed in the drama series *The Lieutenant*?
   a. Camp Pendleton
   b. Camp Peppernick
   c. Camp Pennypacker
   d. Camp Pennsbury

188) In what lawyer series of the early 1960's did Jacob Erlich serve as a consultant?

189) The character of Jonathan Garvey in the series *Little House on the Prairie* was portrayed by this former Los Angeles Rams star.

190) What was another name for William H. Bonney in the western *The Tall Man*?

. . . Answers

181. c

182. Batman and Robin in *Batman*

183. "Blondie Collins"

184. Woodland Oaks, California

185. *The Little People*

186. Chim

187. a

188. *Sam Benedict*

189. Merlin Olsen

190. Billy the Kid

191) Who was the first pilot in the adventure series *Ripcord*?

192) Who were the two Maverick brothers in the western with the same name?

193) Aunt Margaret's home was located across from what famous palace in the comedy series *The Rogues*?

194) What character had pointed ears and bushy eyebrows in the sitcom *The Munsters*?

195) Besides *Gunsmoke*, what other western premiered in the fall of 1955?

196) What cartoon lion likes the phrase "Heavens to Mergatroyd"?

197) Who portrayed April Dancer in the spy series *The Girl from U.N.C.L.E.*?

198) The show *Meet Mr. McNutley* was changed to what title?
   a. *Professor McNutley Goes to Comstock University*
   b. *Professor McNutley and Wife*
   c. *The College Bowl*
   d. none of these

199) Johnny Madrid Lancer and Scott Lancer were half brothers in the western *Lancer*. True or False.

200) Who was the staff photographer for the *Los Angeles Tribune* in the newspaper series *Lou Grant*?

201) What was the name of the sharp black deputy in the sitcom *Carter Country*?

202) Who was Mama's older sister in the comedy series *Mama*?

. . . Answers

191. Chuck Lambert

192. Bret and Bart Maverick

193. Buckingham Palace

194. Edward "Eddie" Wolfgang Munster

195. *The Life and Legend of Wyatt Earp*

196. Snagglepuss

197. Stefanie Powers

198. d (*The Ray Milland Show*)

199. True

200. Dennis "Animal" Price

201. Sgt. Curtis Baker

202. Aunt Jenny

203) Who was Ted Baxter's girlfriend and future wife in the sitcom *The Mary Tyler Moore Show*?

204) Who was the operator of Boulder's New York Delicatessen in the sitcom *Mork & Mindy*?

205) What did Josh Randall call his .30-.40 sawed-off carbine in the western *Wanted: Dead or Alive*?

206) What female character frequently exclaimed "God'll get you for that !"?

207) How many different ranks was Joe Gallagher given in the war drama *Twelve O'Clock High*?
  a. one
  b. two
  c. three
  d. four

208) What character did Frank DeVol portray in the *Fernwood 2-Night* series?

209) What TV character said "It's just a pigment of your imagination"?

210) Stacy Keach portrayed a CONTROL scientist in the sitcom *Get Smart*. True or False?

211) Hugh Brannum portrayed what character friend of Captain Kangaroo?

212) What was the first name of Kelly Gregg's girlfriend in *Bachelor Father*?

213) What was the name of the girls' camp in the sitcom *Camp Runamuck*?

. . . *Answers*

203. Georgette Franklin

204. Remo DaVinci

205. Mare's Leg

206. Maude Findlay, *Maude*

207. c (Captain, Major, and Colonel)

208. Happy Kyne

209. Archie Bunker

210. True

211. Mr. Green Jeans

212. Ginger

213. Camp Divine

214) What was the name of Glen Morley's mother who was portrayed by Cathleen Nesbitt in *The Farmer's Daughter*?

215) What was the name of the orphaned girl saved from a stagecoach mishap by Sam Buckhart in the western *Law of the Plainsman*?

216) What was the name of the community in which Sock Miller sold real estate in the sitcom *The People's Choice*?
    a. Tannersville
    b. Bartonville
    c. Barkerville
    d. Hooterville

217) Who was the commander of the Battlestar Galactica in the science fiction series with the same name?

218) What company did Peter Christopher work for in the sitcom *Occasional Wife*?

219) Who was John King's young sidekick in the crime series *King of Diamonds*?

220) What was the name of the female captain who headed the nurses in the war series *Black Sheep Squadron*?

221) What was Sharon Claridge's role in the police series *Adam-12*?

222) Who was Peter Gunn's singer girlfriend in the detective series *Peter Gunn*?
    a. Sharon
    b. Edie
    c. Eileen
    d. May

. . . *Answers*

214. Agatha

215. Tess Logan

216. c

217. Commander Adama

218. Brahms Baby Food Company

219. Al Casey

220. Capt. Dottie Dixon

221. Dispatcher's voice

222. b

223) In which police series would an announcer describe trial outcomes following the apprehension of the criminal at the conclusion of each episode?

224) What actor portrayed Rudy Jordache in the *Rich Man, Poor Man* series?

225) The Green Hornet's car was a rebuilt 1966 Chrysler Imperial in the crime series *The Green Hornet*. True or False?

226) Who did Commander Donovan replace in the adventure series *The Blue Angels*?

227) What actress portrayed Mama in the sitcom *What's Happening*?

228) Who was Nero Wolfe's trusted assistant in the detective series *Nero Wolfe*?

229) Who was the captain of the *Enterprise* in the adventure series *Riverboat*?

230) What actor portrayed Lurch in the sitcom *The Addams Family*?

231) Where was Jeannie born in the sitcom *I Dream of Jeannie*?

232) What was the name of Dr. Marsh Tracy's daughter in the adventure series *Daktari*?

233) Alexander Scott was a Rhodes Scholar in the adventure series *I Spy*. True or False?

234) What is the name of Fonzie's little cousin, referred to as a nephew, in the sitcom *Happy Days*?

. . . *Answers*

223. *Dragnet*

224. Peter Strauss

225. True

226. Cdr. Arthur Richards

227. Mabel King

228. Archie Goodwin

229. Grey Holden

230. Ted Cassidy

231. Baghdad

232. Paula

233. True

234. Spike

235) To the nearest hundred, how many episodes were made of the western *Death Valley Days*?
    a. 300
    b. 400
    c. 500
    d. 600

236) Who replaced Daniel Briggs as leader of the I.M. Force in the intrigue series *Mission: Impossible*?

237) What was Joe the Bartender's song in *The Jackie Gleason Show*?

238) What actress portrayed the gym teacher, Miss Wilson, in the sitcom *The John Forsythe Show*?

239) Who was the president of the OK Oil Company in the sitcom *The Beverly Hillbillies*?

240) Gladys Ormphby, who like to clout Arte Johnson with her purse in *Rowan & Martin's Laugh In*, was played by what actress?

241) In the *Star Trek* series, how long in terms of years was the "mission" to last?

242) How many episodes comprised the half-hour *Honeymooners* series?
    a. 38
    b. 39
    c. 40
    d. 41

243) What was located on the sole of Maxwell Smart's shoe in the sitcom *Get Smart*?

244) Who was the sheriff in the western *Hec Ramsey*?

. . . Answers

235. d

236. James Phelps

237. "My Gal Sal"

238. Ann B. Davis

239. John Brewster

240. Ruth Buzzi

241. Five-year mission

242. b

243. dial phone

244. Sheriff Oliver B. Stamp

QUESTIONS

245) Who was the half-breed youth in the western *The High Chaparral*?

246) What was the name of the servant and cook in the sitcom *Soap*?

247) What actor portrayed Tom "Sugarfoot" Brewster in the western *Sugarfoot*?

248) What announcer spoke with his hand cupped to his ear in the comedy series *Rowan & Martin's Laugh-In*?

249) What actor in *The Brady Bunch* series became a teen idol during the course of the show?

250) What uncle lived with the Goldbergs in the sitcom of the same name?

251) How was the Bionic Woman injured before she gained superhuman capabilities in the adventure series *The Bionic Woman*?

252) Kookie attained a position as a partner in the featured detective firm of *77 Sunset Strip*. True or False?

253) Who was the sponsor of the police series *The F.B.I.*?

254) Name Wyatt Earp's two brothers wounded in the famous gunfight at the O.K. Corral in *The Life and Legend of Wyatt Earp*.

255) Who first portrayed Chester A. Riley in the sitcom *The Life of Riley*?

256) What music giant was credited with the "manufacture" of the Monkees in the sitcom with the same name?

. . . *Answers*

245. Wind

246. Benson

247. Will Hutchins

248. Gary Owens

249. Barry Williams

250. Uncle David

251. Skydiving accident

252. True

253. Ford Motor Company

254. Morgan and Virgil

255. Jackie Gleason

256. Don Kirshner

257) What was country singer Mac Davis's theme song in the series *The Mac Davis Show*?

258) What character on *M*A*S*H* was best known for his female attire?

259) What was the original title of the documentary series *Animal World*?

260) What actor portrayed Steve Douglas in the sitcom *My Three Sons*?

261) What was the name of Mr. Wilson's dog in the *Dennis the Menace* series?

262) Jim and Joan Nash had two girls and two boys in the sitcom *Please Don't Eat the Daisies*. True or False?

263) Who hosted the *Alcoa Premiere* drama series?

264) "Man-Woman-Birth-Death-Infinity" was the opening line of what medical series?
   a. *Marcus Welby, M.D.*
   b. *Medical Center*
   c. *Dr. Kildare*
   d. *Ben Casey*

265) What was the name of the girls' grandfather in the sitcom *To Rome with Love*?

266) Who sang the theme song "Secret Agent Man" in the series *Secret Agent*?

267) What three westerns did the umbrella title of *Cheyenne* at one time represent?

. . . Answers

257. "I Believe in Music"

258. Cpl. Maxwell Klinger

259. *Animal Kingdom*

260. Fred MacMurray

261. Freemont

262. False, they had four boys

263. Fred Astaire

264. d

265. Grandpa Andy Pruitt

266. Johnny Rivers

267. *Cheyenne, Sugarfoot*, and *Bronco*

268) What show featured this mime team in a skit as the robots "The Clinkers"?

269) A wild story about Ken Osmond (Eddie Haskel of *Leave it to Beaver*) was circulated which claimed he became what rock star?

270) What was the Inspector's name in the adventure series *The Saint*?

271) In what police series were Det. Lt. Ben Guthrie and Inspector Matt Grebb featured?

272) MEtropolis 6-0500 was the phone number of what newspaper in what series?

273) What was the name of the lead character portrayed by John Payne in the western *The Restless Gun*?

274) What was the name of Sam Jones's son in the sitcom *Mayberry, R.F.D.*?
   a. Ed
   b. Mike
   c. Tom
   d. Dan

275) What actress played the part of Helen Roper in the sitcom *The Ropers*?

276) Who were the original three sons of Steve Douglas in the sitcom *My Three Sons*?

277) Who was the Dodge City undertaker in the western *Gunsmoke*?

278) What cartoon character likes the phrase "Thuffering Thucatash"?

. . . Answers

268. *Shields and Yarnell*

269. Alice Cooper

270. Inspector Claude Teal

271. *The Lineup*

272. Daily Planet newspaper, *Superman*

273. Vint Bonner

274. b

275. Audra Lindley

276. Mike, Robbie, and Chip

277. Percy Crump

278. Sylvester the Cat

279) Who was the surfer who gave Francine Lawrence her nickname in the series *Gidget*?

280) What actor portrayed Jim Quince in the western series *Rawhide*?

281) Buelah was the name of the witch in the children's series *Kukla, Fran & Ollie*. True or False?

282) What were the names of Lucy Carmichael's two children who lived with her in Danfield, Connecticut in the sitcom *The Lucy Show*?

283) Who played Pasquinel in the drama series *Centennial*?

284) In what city did the M Squad combat crime in the police series with the same name?
   a. Philadelphia
   b. Chicago
   c. Detroit
   d. Miami

285) In what small Ohio town did Mary Hartman live in the soap *Mary Hartman, Mary Hartman*?

286) What were the names of Jerry and Susie Hubbard Buells' twins in the sitcom *The Mothers-in-Law*?

287) Who did John Travolta portray in the sitcom *Welcome Back, Kotter*?

288) What was the name of the production company formed by Desi Arnaz and Lucille Ball?

289) Astronaut Tony Nelson was a Major when the *I Dream of Jeannie* series started. True or False?

. . . Answers

279. Jeff Matthews or "Moon Doggie"

280. Steve Raines

281. True

282. Chris and Jerry

283. Robert Conrad

284. b

285. Fernwood

286. Hildy and Joey

287. Vinnie Barbarino

288. Desilu Productions

289. False, he was a Captain

290) What was the name of the young photographer in the western *Cimarron Strip*?

291) ". . . and you, have you ever been there?" was part of the closing narration in what science fiction anthology?

292) The Evil Queen of Cygnil and the Mad Witch of Neptune were two of the enemies of which science fiction hero of the 1950's?

293) What was Andy's street address in Mayberry in *The Andy Griffith Show*?

294) What was the name of the "Hat Check Girl" at the Ma-Combo Club in the sitcom *The George Burns and Gracie Allen Show*?

295) In *The Courtship of Eddie's Father*, what actress portrayed Mrs. Livingston?

296) What was the office number of Barnaby Jones in the series with the same name?

297) What was the name of Captain Video's spacecraft in the children's series *Captain Video and His Video Rangers*?

298) What was Betty Anderson's nickname on the sitcom *Father Knows Best*?

299) Who was the popular mustachioed violinist of *The Lawrence Welk Show*?
   a. Jerry Burke
   b. Dick Dale
   c. Myron Floren
   d. Aladdin

. . . *Answers*

290. Francis Wilde

291. *The Twilight Zone*

292. Flash Gordon, *Flash Gordon*

293. 14 Maple St.

294. Vickie Donavan

295. Miyoshi Umeki

296. 615

297. *Galaxy*

298. Princess

299. d

300) "Come On, Get Happy" was the theme song of what sitcom of the early 1970's?

301) What was the name of the high school principal in the sitcom *The Bill Cosby Show*?

302) Who was Felix Unger's daughter in the sitcom *The Odd Couple*?

303) What character did Vince Conti portray in the police series *Kojak*?

304) Kelly Gregg and Warren Dawson were married in the sitcom *Bachelor Father*. True or False?

305) "Have you figured it out? Do you know who the murderer is?" are lines from which detective series?

306) Who was Tony Petrocelli's cowboy investigator in the lawyer series *Petrocelli*?

307) What musical variety show, first telecast in January of 1976, featured a teenaged brother and sister co-host team?

308) Bluto was another name for what cartoon character in the *Popeye* cartoons?

309) What was the name of Ralph Henley's son in the adventure series *The Greatest American Hero*?
   a. Brian
   b. Billy
   c. Todd
   d. Kevin

310) To what variety series would the following telecasts be associated: "One Day in the Life of Ivan Denisovich," "The Seven Little Foys," and "Think Pretty"?

. . . Answers

300. *The Partridge Family*

301. Mr. Langford

302. Edna

303. Detective Rizzo

304. False

305. *Ellery Queen*

306. Pete Ritter

307. *Donny & Marie*

308. Brutus

309. d

310. *Bob Hope Presents the Chrysler Theatre*

311) What were the streetwise students in the sitcom *Welcome Back Kotter* called?

312) Who was Dick and Jenny Preston's daughter in the sitcom *The New Dick Van Dyke Show*?

313) Who was "the Texan" in the western with the same name?

314) 0001 North Cemetery Ridge was the home address of what sitcom family?

315) Mrs. MacGillicuddy always called Ricky Ricardo "Mickey" in the *I Love Lucy* shows. True or False?

316) Who was the Williamses' housekeeper in the sitcom *Make Room for Daddy*?

317) What was the name of Alexander Mundy's boss during the first season of the intrigue series *It Takes a Thief*?

318) What was the theme song of the western *Have Gun Will Travel*?

319) Who was Dean Martin's pianist in *The Dean Martin Show*?

320) At what high school did John Novak teach in the drama series *Mr. Novak*?
  a. Jefferson High
  b. Henderson High
  c. East High
  d. Great Valley High

321) What was Tom Jones's theme song which was recorded in 1967?

. . . Answers

311. "Sweathogs"

312. Annie

313. Bill Longley

314. *The Addams Family*

315. True

316. Louise

317. Noah Bain

318. "Ballad of Paladin"

319. Ken Lane

320. a

321. "It's Not Unusual"

QUESTIONS

322) "The Brother-in-Law" was a sketch featured on what comedy variety series which was first telecast in the fall of 1969?

323) What did the Clampetts call their swimming pool in the sitcom *The Beverly Hillbillies*?

324) What was a "walnetto" in the comedy variety series *Rowan & Martin's Laugh-In*?
   a. kiss
   b. candy
   c. hug
   d. drink

325) What was Captain Kirk's nickname for Dr. Leonard McCoy in the science fiction series *Star Trek*?

326) Ralph and Ed of *The Honeymooners* bowl on alley number five. True or False?

327) What is the name of the Flintstones' newspaper in the cartoon series *The Flintstones*?

328) Who was Dick Hollister's employer in the sitcom *He & She*?

329) What was Hogan's code name in the sitcom *Hogan's Heroes*?

330) Who was the chief medical officer in the science fiction series *Space: 1999*?

331) What was the name of Thomas Hewitt Edward Cat's Spanish gypsy friend in the adventure series *T.H.E. Cat*?

332) Who was Chicken George's mother in the drama series *Roots*?

. . . Answers

322. *The Jim Nabors Hour*

323. "The cement pond"

324. b

325. "Bones"

326. False, number three

327. *Bedrock Gazette*

328. Norman Nugent

329. Papa Bear

330. Dr. Helena Russell

331. Pepe

332. Kizzy

333) What two religious groups were represented by the Steinberg couple in *Bridget Loves Bernie*?

334) On what comedy show of the late 1970's did the Unknown Comic appear with a paper bag over his head?

335) Who was the Bumsteads' mailman in the sitcom *Blondie*?

336) What was Kookie's word for the "greatest" in the detective series *77 Sunset Srip*?

337) What was the name of Doug Lawrence's wife in the drama series *Family*?
    a. Rose
    b. Lee
    c. Mary
    d. Kate

338) What friend of Wally's enjoyed calling Beaver a "squirt" in the sitcom *Leave it to Beaver*?

339) In 1960's jargon, whose "pad" was located at 1438 North Beachwood Drive in a sitcom series?

340) Max was the name of Mike Longstreet's seeing eye dog in the detective series *Longstreet*. True or False?

341) What was the name of Sue Ann Niven's television program on station WJM in the sitcom *The Mary Tyler Moore Show*?

342) What was the name of Katy O'Connor's roommate in the sitcom *The Ann Sothern Show*?

343) Who was Steve Douglas's father-in-law in the sitcom *My Three Sons*?

. . . *Answers*

333. Bridget (Catholics) and Bernie (Jews)

334. *The Gong Show*

335. Mr. Beasley

336. "Ginchiest"

337. d

338. Eddie Haskell

339. The Monkees, *The Monkees*

340. False, Pax

341. "Happy Homemaker Show"

342. Olive Smith

343. "Bub" O'Casey

344) What TV father was employed by Trask Engineering?

345) Who did Phyllis Lindstrom live with in the sitcom *Phyllis*?

346) What actor portrayed Jingles in the western *The Adventures of Wild Bill Hickok*?

347) What was the name of Bruce Wayne's (Batman's) housekeeper in the *Batman* adventure series?

348) From what state was Professor Michael Endicott in the sitcom *To Rome with Love*?
    a. Kansas
    b. Ohio
    c. Iowa
    d. Missouri

349) What character did Lee Majors portray in the adventure series *The Six Million Dollar Man*?

350) What was the name of Princess Ardala's henchman in the science fiction series *Buck Rogers in the 25th Century*?

351) What rock 'n' roll show of the mid 1960's starred Sam Cooke in its premiere and the Rolling Stones in its second season?

352) The characters of Doc Fabrique and Doc Holliday were portrayed by the same actor in the western *The Life and Legend of Wyatt Earp*. True or False?

353) What was the name of the goat featured in the sitcom *Sanford and Son*?

354) Who were the Ingalls' three daughters at the start of the *Little House on the Prairie* series?

. . . Answers

344. Henry Mitchell, *Dennis the Menace*

345. Mother-in-law, Audrey Dexter

346. Andy Devine

347. Aunt Harriet

348. c

349. Col. Steve Austin

350. Kane

351. *Shindig*

352. True, Douglas Fowley

353. Ninny

354. Mary, Laura, and Carrie

QUESTIONS

355) Praetor was associated with the Klingons in the science fiction series *Star Trek*. True or False?

356) Who did Jim Davis portray in the adventure series *Rescue 8*?

357) What hero of a police series, which aired throughout most of the 1970s, liked the phrase "There you go"?

358) How many "Rough Riders" were there in the western series with the same name?

359) What was the name of the elevator operator in the sitcom *My Little Margie*?

360) What was the name of the malt shop in the sitcom *Happy Days*?

361) Who did the cartoon character Wile E. Coyote pursue?

362) Britt Reid (Green Hornet) was the great-grandnephew of the Lone Ranger in *The Green Hornet* crime series. True or False?

363) What character did Ray Bolger portray in the sitcom *The Ray Bolger Show*?

364) What was the name of the brewery which employed Laverne & Shirley in the sitcom with the same name?

365) What character composed menus for a living in the sitcom *Love on a Rooftop*?

366) Who was the oldest of the Cartwright sons in the western *Bonanza*?

. . . *Answers*

355. False, the Romulans

356. Wes Cameron

357. Sam McCloud, *McCloud*

358. Three

359. Charlie

360. Arnold's Drive-In

361. The Roadrunner

362. True

363. Raymond Wallace

364. Shotz Brewery

365. Stan Parker

366. Adam Cartwright

367) In what city was U.N.C.L.E.'s American headquarters located in the spy series *The Man from U.N.C.L.E.*?
    a. Chicago
    b. Atlanta
    c. New York
    d. Los Angeles

368) Robert Ironside's would-be assassin was a woman in the police series *Ironside*. True or False?

369) What cattle rancher was also the mayor of Cimarron City in the western with the same last name?

370) What were the names of agent West's two horses in the series *The Wild Wild West*?

371) Who was Mark Saber's assistant in the detective series *Inspector Mark Saber - Homicide Squad*?

372) What character was portrayed by Desi Arnaz in the sitcom *The Mothers-in-Law*?

373) What type of car did Dan Tanna drive in the detective series *Vegas*?

374) Cowtown, Texas was the hometown of which female sitcom character whose first show was telecast in March of 1980?

375) Where did Barney Fife keep his "allowed" one bullet in the sitcom *The Andy Griffith Show*?

376) What state was home for the black bear Ben in the adventure series *Gentle Ben*?
    a. Pennsylvania
    b. Maine
    c. New Hampshire
    d. Florida

. . . Answers

367. c

368. True, Honor Thompson

369. Matthew Rockford

370. Duke and Cacao

371. Sgt. Tim Maloney

372. Raphael del Gado

373. Red Thunderbird

374. Florence Jean Castleberry, *Flo*

375. left breast pocket

376. d

377) In what state was the town of Centennial located in the series with the same name?

378) What was the theme song of the children's series *The Banana Splits*?

379) Who portrayed Frank Cannon in the detective series *Cannon*?

380) What was the name of the Martin's family dog in the sitcom *The Doris Day Show*?

381) What actor portrayed Abraham Lincoln Jones in the lawyer series *The Law and Mr. Jones*?

382) What was the name of the young law partner portrayed by Lee Majors in the lawyer series *Owen Marshall, Counselor at Law*?

383) What were the names of Goldie Appleby's two ex-roommates in the sitcom *The Betty Hutton Show*?

384) Felix Unger was a television newswriter in the sitcom *The Odd Couple*. True or False?

385) What was the name of Kaz's girlfriend in the lawyer series with the same name?

386) What character did William Shatner portray in the western *The Barbary Coast*?

387) Occasional appearances were made by Hank Peterson who portrayed which character in the western *The Adventures of Kit Carson*?

    a. Rough Rider   c. Rugged Rancher
    b. El Toro   d. Sierra Jack

. . . Answers

377. Colorado

378. "Tra-la-la Song"

379. William Conrad

380. Lord Nelson

381. James Whitmore

382. Jess Brandon

383. Lorna and Rosemary

384. False, a photographer

385. Katie McKenna

386. Jeff Cable

387. d

388) Who was the vice-president of the C.F. & W. Railroad in the sitcom *Petticoat Junction*?

389) What character did Dick Van Patten portray in the comedy series *Eight is Enough*?

390) What female character of a sitcom of the late 1950's and early 1960's was called "Sugar Babe" by her husband?

391) What was the name of the Douglases' cow in the sitcom *Green Acres*?

392) Who was the airline pilot who occasionally gave Bob and Emily miniature bottles of liquor in the sitcom *The Bob Newhart Show*?

393) Who was the first principal in the drama series *The White Shadow*?

394) What heart transplant specialist was replaced by Dr. Martin Cohen in the medical series *The New Doctors*?

395) Tom Jordache was a wrestler in the mini series *Rich Man, Poor Man - Book I*. True or False?

396) What was the name of the cousin in the sitcom *The Addams Family*?

397) Other than Capt. Tony Nelson, what other character knew about Jeannie in the sitcom *I Dream of Jeannie*?

398) "Best Friend" was the theme song of this sitcom which starred Bill Bixby and Brandon Cruz.

399) What was the name of Dr. Peter Brady's sister in the intrigue series *The Invisible Man*?

... *Answers*

388. Homer Bedloe

389. Tom Bradford

390. Kate McCoy of *The Real McCoys*

391. Elinor

392. Howard Borden

393. Jim Willis

394. Dr. Ted Stuart

395. False, a boxer

396. Cousin Itt

397. Capt. Roger Healey

398. *The Courtship of Eddie's Father*

399. Diane Brady

400) In the western series *Have Gun Will Travel*, what was the Paladin's logo?
   a. chess knight
   b. chess king
   c. chess queen
   d. chess bishop

401) What was the name of Buddy Sorrell's wife in the sitcom *The Dick Van Dyke Show*?

402) Who was Millie's romantic interest in the sitcom *Meet Millie*?

403) What was the name of the famous dancers in *The Jackie Gleason Show*?

404) "And good night Mrs. Calabash, wherever you are" was the closing line of what comedy variety series of the mid 1950's?

405) What was the name of the town where the Clampetts lived before their move to Beverly Hills in the sitcom *The Beverly Hillbillies*?

406) What was Joseph Rockford's (Jim Rockford's father) nickname in the detective series *The Rockford Files*?

407) Barbara Feldon had won $64,000 on the quiz show *The $64,000 Question* in the literature category with her knowledge of which author?

408) What was the name of Victoria Cannon's brother in the western *The High Chaparral*?

409) What was the name of Maxwell Smart's dog in the sitcom *Get Smart*?

. . . Answers

400. a

401. Pickles

402. Johnny Boone, Jr.

403. June Taylor Dancers

404. *The Jimmy Durante Show*

405. Bug Tussell

406. Rocky

407. Shakespeare

408. Manolito Montoya

409. Fang or K-13

410) White Lace Mountain was the location of the Bolts' wooded land in the comedy series *Here Come the Brides*. True or False?

411) What was the name of the lodge that Ralph Kramden and Ed Norton joined in the sitcom *The Honeymooners*?

412) What was the name of the research colony in the science fiction series *Space: 1999*?

413) Who were the three young detectives featured in the series *Surfside Six*?

414) Who was David McKay's romantic interest in the drama series *Operation: Runaway*?

415) Sheriff Roy Coffee was the sheriff of what city in the western *Bonanza*?
    a. Dodge City
    b. Oklahoma City
    c. Virginia City
    d. Kansas City

416) This show, which starred Jim Nabors, was a spin-off of *The Andy Griffith Show*.

417) What was the name of Victoria Barkley's horse in the western *The Big Valley*?

418) What was Jessica's father known as in the sitcom *Soap*?

419) Among the characters portrayed by Mr. Magoo in the cartoon series *The Famous Adventures of Mr. Magoo* were Long John Silver and Friar Tuck. True or False?

420) Who produced *The Mothers-in-Law*?

. . . *Answers*

410. False, Bridal Veil Mountain

411. Royal Order of Raccoons

412. Moonbase Alpha

413. Ken Madison, Dave Thorne, and Sandy Winfield II

414. Karen Wingate

415. c

416. *Gomer Pyle, U.S.M.C.*

417. Misty Girl

418. "the Major"

419. True

420. Desi Arnaz

421) What teenaged sitcom character made this statment: ". . . I love girls. I'm not a wolf, mind you. A wolf wants lots of girls. I just want one . . . lousy girl."

422) What was the name given to the North Korean pilot who was determined to bomb the M.A.S.H. unit in the *M*A*S*H* series?

423) What was the name of George Apple's wife in the drama series *Apple's Way*?

424) What actor portrayed Det. Lt. Mike Haines in the police series *N.Y.P.D.*?

425) What did Dennis like to keep in his back pocket in the sitcom *Dennis the Menace*?

426) Who was the Nashes' maid in the sitcom *Please Don't Eat the Daisies*?

427) How many actors portrayed the teenaged character Henry Aldrich in the sitcom *The Aldrich Family*?

428) Who was the police commissioner of Gotham City in the adventure series *Batman*?

429) Who was Harry Lime's occasional assistant in the intrigue series *The Third Man*?

430) What was Jon Bauman's nickname in the musical variety show *Sha Na Na*?

431) Ranakai Island was the location of the military base in the sitcom *Broadside*. True or False?

432) What character did John Bromfield portray in the police series *The Sheriff of Cochise*?

. . . Answers

421. Dobie Gillis, *The Many Loves of Dobie Gillis*

422. 5 O'Clock Charlie

423. Barbara

424. Jack Warden

425. Slingshot

426. Martha O'Reilly

427. Five

428. Commissioner James W. Gordon

429. Bradford Webster

430. "Bowzer"

431. True

432. Sheriff Frank Morgan

433) What was the name of Elizabeth's husband in the sitcom *Life with Elizabeth*?

    a. Mark

    b. Clyde

    c. Alvin

    d. Frank

434) What was the name of the fireman whom Beaver frequently chatted with in the sitcom *Leave it to Beaver*?

435) What was the name of the rooming house run by Aunt Esther in the sitcom *Sanford & Son*?

436) In this adventure series, Tic Toc Base was the secret location of what type of machine, the type of machine also being the name of the series?

437) What was the name of Frank McBride's pet plant in the detective series *Switch*?

438) What was the name of the club where Pinky Pinkham worked in the newspaper series *The Roaring Twenties*?

439) At the start of the final season of *McHale's Navy*, where were McHale and his crew transferred?

440) Where was the Ropers' town house located in the sitcom *The Ropers*?

441) What was the name of Mrs. Maggie Davis's cat in the sitcom *Our Miss Brooks*?

442) Who replaced Arnold as the owner of Arnold's Drive-In in the sitcom *Happy Days*?

443) What is the name of Yogi Bear's little bear sidekick?

. . . Answers

433. c

434. Gus

435. Sanford Arms

436. *The Time Tunnel*

437. Herbert

438. Charleston Club

439. Voltafiore, Italy

440. Cheviot Hills

441. Minerva

442. Alfred Delvecchio

443. Boo Boo

QUESTIONS

444) In *Gilligan's Island*, what character was portrayed by Jim Backus, whose voice is that of Mr. Magoo?

445) What was the name of the German Commanding Officer whose forces usually opposed the "Rat Patrol" in the series *The Rat Patrol*?

446) To what company did the Texas Rangers of the western *Laredo* belong?
   a. Company A
   b. Company B
   c. Company C
   d. Company D

447) The Robinson family was destined for a planet in what star system before they became "lost in space" in the science fiction series *Lost in Space*?

448) What actress portrayed the Bionic Woman in the adventure series *The Bionic Woman*?

449) Who was the "man" against crime in the detective series with the same name?

450) What was the name of Howdy Doody's sister in the children's series *Howdy Doody Time*?

451) What actor portrayed the Police Inspector in the adventure series *China Smith*?

452) What evil genius, portrayed by dwarf Michael Dunn, was the enemy of James T. West in the western *The Wild Wild West*?

453) Who was WJM-TV's weatherman in the sitcom *The Mary Tyler Moore Show*?

. . . Answers

444. Thurston Howell III

445. Capt. Hauptman Hans Dietrich

446. b

447. Alpha Centauri

448. Lindsay Wagner

449. Mike Barnett

450. Heidi Doody

451. Douglas Dumbrille

452. Dr. Miguelito Loveless

453. Gordon Howard or Gordie

454) What sitcom family lived at 1313 Mockingbird Lane in Mockingbird Heights?

455) Who hosted *The Twilight Zone*?

456) Coral Key Park was the featured park in the adventure series *Flipper*. True or False?

457) What was Archie's favorite hangout in the sitcom *All in the Family*?

458) "That Wonderful Year" was a highlight of what variety show which was first telecast in the fall of 1958?

459) Who was the captain of the 53rd Precinct in the sitcom *Car 54, Where Are You*?

460) What police detective resided at the King Edward Hotel?

461) Which of the following characters was not an adversary of Captain Video in the children's series *Captain Video and His Video Rangers*?
     a. Nargola
     b. Mook the Moon Man
     c. Heng Foo Seeng
     d. Frog Man

462) Other than Rob and Laura Petrie, who was the other featured "couple" (unmarried) in the sitcom *The Dick Van Dyke Show*?

463) Who was Rhoda's mother in the sitcom *The Mary Tyler Moore Show*?

464) Who was Patty Lane's father in the sitcom *The Patty Duke Show*?

. . . Answers

454. The Munsters, *The Munsters*

455. Rod Serling

456. True

457. Kelcy's Bar

458. *The Garry Moore Show*

459. Captain Block

460. Tony Baretta, *Baretta*

461. d

462. Buddy Sorrell and Sally Rogers

463. Ida Morgenstern

464. Martin Lane

QUESTIONS

465) What character did actresses Butterfly McQueen and Ruby Dandridge portray in the sitcom *Beulah*?

466) What were the two English neighbors of Felix and Oscar known as in the sitcom *The Odd Couple*?

467) What quiz show of the late 1950's was at different times emceed by Monty Hall, Carl Reiner, and Merv Griffin?

468) What actress portrayed Maggie Rogers in the mini-series *Backstairs at the White House*?

469) What hotel did Clay Baker manage in the *Adventures in Paradise* series?

470) Who was Perry Mason's secretary in the lawyer series with the same name?

471) What was the name of the Stones' adopted daughter who joined the household in 1963 in the sitcom *The Donna Reed Show*?

472) What is the name of the Sea Hag's vulture in the *Popeye* cartoons?

473) Ralph Henley was a news anchorman in the adventure series *The Greatest American Hero*. True or False?

474) What other character did Bob Cummings portray in the sitcom *Love that Bob*, other than the role of Bob Collins?

475) Who was Roger's pesky little sister in the sitcom *What's Happening*?

476) What character did Francis De Sales portray in the comedy series *Mr. and Mrs. North*?

. . . Answers

465. Oriole, Beulah's girlfriend

466. Pigeon Sisters

467. *Keep Talking*

468. Olivia Cole

469. Bali Miki Hotel

470. Della Street

471. Trisha Stone

472. Bernard

473. False, a teacher

474. Josh Collins or Grandpa (Bob's father)

475. Dee

476. Lt. Bill Weigand

477) Who was the cab company's mechanic in the sitcom *Taxi*?

478) What was the name of the pet lion in the sitcom *The Addams Family*?

479) What actor portrayed Special Agent Jerry Dressler in the intrigue series *I Led Three Lives*?

480) What World War II war series, which starred Rick Jason and Vic Morrow, contained actual battle footage in some episodes?

481) What was the name of the chef in the sitcom *It's a Living*?
    a. Luca
    b. Mario
    c. Francesco
    d. Marco

482) What ws the name of Fonzie's favorite magazine in the sitcom *Happy Days*?
    a. Hot Tracks
    b. Hot Wheels
    c. Hot Rod
    d. Hot Machines

483) What actor narrated the western *The Deputy*?

484) Who was the electronics expert in the intrigue series *Mission: Impossible*?

485) What was the name of the Jetson's son in the cartoon series *The Jetsons*?

486) On what Network was *The Jackie Gleason Show* aired?

. . . *Answers*

477. Latka Gravas

478. Kit Kat

479. John Zaremba

480. *Combat*

481. b

482. c

483. Henry Fonda

484. Barney Collier

485. Elroy

486. CBS

487) The phrase "Here come de judge!" was popularized on what comedy variety series?

488) What actress, who portrayed the nurse Christine Chapel in the science fiction series *Star Trek*, was also the voice of the computer?

489) What was the name of Honey West's partner in the detective series *Honey West*?

490) Who was the captain of F Troop in the sitcom *F Troop*?

491) What was the name of the Baxters' dog in the sitcom *Hazel*?

492) What color tablecloth did the Kramdens have on their round wood table in the sitcom *The Honeymooners*?

493) What musical variety show featured the segments "Vamp" and "Dirty Linen"?

494) Other than *The Tonight Show*, what other comedy variety series featured the "Man-on-the-Street Interview"?

495) Toby had lost a hand in the drama series *Roots*. True or False?

496) How many bedrooms did the Brady house have in the sitcom *The Brady Bunch*?
  a. four
  b. five
  c. six
  d. seven

497) What character did Sally Field portray in the sitcom *The Girl with Something Extra*?

. . . Answers

487. *Rowan & Martin's Laugh-In*

488. Majel Barrett

489. Sam Bolt

490. Capt. Wilton Parmenter

491. Smiley

492. Red-and-white-checked

493. *The Sonny and Cher Comedy Hour*

494. *The Steve Allen Show*

495. False, a foot

496. a

497. Sally Burton

498) What was the name of Mr. Dither's wife in the series *Blondie*?

499) Who were the two featured detectives in the series *77 Sunset Strip*?

500) The Nairobi Trio, a regular feature of the comedy series *The Ernie Kovacs Show*, consisted of three musical witch doctors. True or False?

501) What was the name of the notorious doctor in the western *The Life and Legend of Wyatt Earp*?

502) Which of the two families featured in the sitcom *The Mothers-in-Law* was the unconventional one?

503) What was the name of the gang that ambushed the Texas Rangers in the western *The Lone Ranger*?

504) What was the name of the group of young singers who became regulars on *The Andy Williams Show* from 1962 through 1971?

505) Who was Vernon Albright's romantic interest in the sitcom *My Little Margie*?

506) What was Dennis the Menace's favorite drink in the sitcom *Dennis the Menace*?
   a. milk
   b. grape juice
   c. orange juice
   d. root beer

507) What character did Maurice Gosfield portray in the sitcom *The Phil Silvers Show: You'll Never Get Rich*?

... Answers

498. Cora

499. Stuart Bailey and Jeff Spencer

500. False, three musical gorillas

501. Doc Holliday

502. Buells

503. "Hole-in-the-Wall" gang

504. The Osmond Brothers

505. Roberta Townsend

506. d

507. Pvt. Duane Doberman

508) What character in *The Adventures of Superman* series liked the phrase "Great Caesar's ghost!"?

509) Who were the two scientists locked in the "time tunnel" in the science fiction series with the same name?

510) What instrument did "Screamin' Scott" Simon play on the musical variety show *Sha Na Na*?

511) What actress played the role of the wealthy Mrs. Gruber in the sitcom *The Brian Keith Show*?

512) In what state was Cochise County located in the series *The Sheriff of Cochise*?

513) Who portrayed Chester A. Riley in the second cast in the sitcom *The Life of Riley*?

514) What friend of Wally's was repeatedly sent to the Cleavers to apologize for his actions in the sitcom *Leave it to Beaver*?

515) Who produced the sitcom *Sanford and Son*?

516) Both of Mr. Spock's parents were Vulcans in the science fiction series *Star Trek*. True or False?

517) What were the names of the two reporters in the series *The Roaring Twenties*?

518) Who was the county clerk in the sitcom *Mayberry, R.F.D.*?

519) Margie's schemes were made with this old next-door neighbor portrayed by Gertrude Hoffman in the sitcom *My Little Margie*?

. . . Answers

508. Perry White, newspaper editor

509. Dr. Tony Newman and Dr. Doug Phillips

510. Piano

511. Nancy Kulp

512. Arizona

513. William Bendix

514. Clarence "Lumpy" Rutherford

515. Norman Lear

516. False, his mother was a human

517. Scott Norris and Pat Garrison

518. Howard Sprague

519. Mrs. Odetts

QUESTIONS

520) What was the name of the realtor in the sitcom *The Ropers*?

521) What was the first theme song of the sitcom *Happy Days* which was originally recorded by Bill Haley & The Comets?

522) In what national park does Yogi Bear reside?

523) Aside from serving as first lady, J.J. of *The Governor & J.J.* also worked in what public place?

524) What form of transportation was used by the "Rat Patrol" in the series with the same name?
    a. tanks
    b. armored cars
    c. jeeps
    d. none of these

525) Who was the jet-set heiress in the science fiction series *Land of the Giants*?

526) Who was the young corporal who brooded over his sexual inexperience in the sitcom *M*A*S*H*?

527) Who was Lou Grant's friend and managing editor in the newspaper series *Lou Grant*?

528) Deputy Jasper DeWitt, Jr. was known as the "good ole boy" in the sitcom *Carter Country*. True or False?

529) Elmer was the original name of what famous puppet?

530) What was a female patrolwoman known as in the police series *Chips*?

531) By what name is the character Diana Prince better known?

... *Answers*

520. Jeffrey P. Brookes III

521. "Rock Around the Clock"

522. Jellystone National Park

523. Zoo

524. c

525. Valerie Scott

526. Cpl. Walter "Radar" O'Reilly

527. Charlie Hume

528. True

529. Howdy Doody, *Howdy Doody Time*

530. Chippie

531. Wonder Woman

QUESTIONS

532) Who was Mary Hartman's friend and aspiring country music singer in the soap *Mary Hartman, Mary Hartman*?

533) Who was Mindy's socially and politically oriented cousin in the sitcom *Mork & Mindy*?

534) Who was Cosmo Topper's wife in the sitcom *Topper*?

535) What actress portrayed Fay Stewart in the sitcom *Fay*?

536) Where did Lt. Col. Henry Blake go to college in the *M*A*S*H* series?
   a. University of Wisconsin
   b. University of Georgia
   c. University of Pennsylvania
   d. Univeristy of Illinois

537) Who was Andy's cousin-deputy in the sitcom *The Andy Griffith Show*?

538) What variety series, first telecast in the spring of 1949, had "Sentimental Journey" as its theme song?

539) Who employed the Cloak of Invisibility as a weapon against Captain Video in the children's series *Captain Video and His Video Rangers*?

540) What was the name of the dog in the Gregg household in the sitcom *Bachelor Father*?

541) Dion Patrick was employed as a reporter in the western *The Californians*. True or False?

542) Who ruled the evil planet of Mongo in the science fiction series *Flash Gordon*?

. . . Answers

532. Loretta Haggers

533. Nelson Flavor

534. Henrietta

535. Lee Grant

536. d

537. Barney Fife

538. *Garroway at Large*

539. Dr. Pauli

540. Jasper

541. True

542. Emperor Ming

543) Who did Edna Babish marry in the sitcom *Laverne & Shirley*?

544) Who was the principal of Madison High School in the sitcom *Our Miss Brooks*?

545) What precinct was featured in the sitcom *Barney Miller*?
   a. 12th
   b. 16th
   c. 22nd
   d. 42nd

546) Who was Oscar's secretary in the sitcom *The Odd Couple*?

547) What was the name of the college at which Prof. Ray McNutley taught in the series *Meet Mr. McNutley*?

548) What was the name of the island on which Maj. Gregory "Pappy" Boyington and his men were stationed in the war series *Baa Baa Black Sheep*?

549) Morticia Addams of the sitcom *The Addams Family* was portrayed by what actress?

550) What sitcom was the successor to *December Bride*?

551) What variety show, which spanned over two decades, was originally titled *Toast of the Town*?

552) Who was Castor Oyl's sister in the cartoon series *Popeye*?

553) What actor portrayed Senator Joe Kelley in the sitcom *Grandpa Goes to Washington*?

554) What sitcom of the late 1950's would begin with these lines: "Hold it! I think you're going to like this picture"?

. . . *Answers*

543. Frank DeFazio

544. Osgood Conklin

545. a

546. Myrna Turner

547. Lynnhaven College

548. Vella La Cava

549. Carolyn Jones

550. *Pete and Gladys*

551. *The Ed Sullivan Show*

552. Olive Oyl

553. Jack Albertson

554. *Love That Bob*

555) How many children did John and Olivia Walton have in the drama series *The Waltons*?

    a. five
    b. six
    c. seven
    d. eight

556) What was the name of the quiz show of the early 1950's whose contestants had the same name as a famous person?

557) Who was the wealthy widower in the sitcom *Tammy*?

558) Who was the NASA psychiatrist who found Capt. Tony Nelson's behavior quite peculiar in the sitcom *I Dream of Jeannie*?

559) The prizes in this quiz show appeared behind a 30-square game board and in order to claim the prize, contestants were required to match the two correct squares.

560) An unhealthy dosage of radiation was responsible for David Bruce Banner's physical transformation into the Hulk in the adventure series *The Incredible Hulk*. True or False?

561) What was Fonzie's nickname for Mrs. Cunningham in the sitcom *Happy Days*?

562) What feature of *The Dean Martin Comedy Hour* proved so popular that it was carried over into a series of occasional specials?

563) What ad agency did Joey Barnes work for during the first season of *The Joey Bishop Show*?

564) What character replaced Albert Vane as the principal in the series *Mr. Novak*?

. . . Answers

555. c

556. *The Name's the Same*

557. John Brent

558. Dr. Alfred Bellows

559. *Concentration*

560. True

561. Mrs. C.

562. "Man of the Week Celebrity Roast"

563. Wellington, Willoughby, and Jones

564. Martin Woodridge

565) What was the name of the musical variety show which starred the country singer known for his famous single "Big Bad John"?

566) What was Granny's full character name in the sitcom *The Beverly Hillbillies*?

567) What was the name of the principal in the *Room 222* series?

568) What was the name of Dino's Restaurant's parking lot attendant in the detective series *77 Sunset Strip*?

569) Who was the ranch foreman in the western *The High Chaparral*?

570) Who is Fred Flintstone's boss in the cartoon series *The Flinstones*?

571) On what network was the detective series *Hawaiian Eye* telecast?
    a. ABC
    b. NBC
    c. CBS
    d. ABC and NBC

572) What was the name of the wealthy family in the sitcom *Soap*?

573) What was Hazel's address when she lived with George and Dorothy Baxter in the sitcom *Hazel*?

574) Who was the state trooper in the police series *State Trooper*?

575) What character did Linc Case replace in the adventure series *Route 66*?

. . . Answers

565. *The Jimmy Dean Show*

566. Daisy Moses

567. Seymour Kaufman

568. Kookie, later replaced by J. R. Hale

569. Sam Butler

570. Mr. Slate

571. a

572. Tates

573. 123 Marshall Rd., Hydesberg, NY

574. Trooper Rod Blake

575. Buzz Murdock

576) Alice, the Bradys' housekeeper in the sitcom *The Brady Bunch*, had a boyfriend who was a car salesman. True or False?

577) Where was the Goldberg's favorite summer retreat in the sitcom *The Goldbergs*?

578) What were the names of Dagwood and Blondie's two children in the sitcom *Blondie*?

579) How old was Luke Carpenter when he became frozen in an avalanche in the sitcom *The Second Hundred Years*?
    a. 30
    b. 31
    c. 32
    d. 33

580) What character played nanny to the three young orphans in the sitcom *Family Affair*?

581) What was the name of Chester Riley's daughter in the series *The Life of Riley*?

582) Who portrayed Angie Falco Benson in the sitcom *Angie*?

583) What was the name of Mike's fiancée in the sitcom *My Three Sons*?

584) What type of "watching" did George Wilson like to engage in during some episodes of the sitcom *Dennis the Menace*?

585) What was the name of the Nashes' dog in the sitcom *Please Don't Eat the Daisies*?
    a. Ladadog
    b. Freemont
    c. Ralph
    d. Captain

... Answers

576. False, Sam was a butcher

577. Pincus Pines in the Catskills

578. Alexander and Cookie

579. d

580. Mr. (Giles) French

581. Babs

582. Donna Pescow

583. Sally Ann Morrison

584. Bird watching

585. a

586) Who was the sponsor of the sitcom *The Aldrich Family*?

587) What character did Lee Meriwether portray in the science fiction series *The Time Tunnel*?

588) "On, King! On, you huskies" was a familiar line on what police adventure series?

589) What western of the later 1950's was based on Elliott Arnold's novel *Blood Brother*?

590) Who played the part of Shotgun Slade in the western with the same name?

591) What sitcom couple had four redheaded sons?

592) Who was Wyatt's deputy in Tombstone in the western *The Life and Legend of Wyatt Earp*?

593) Who played the part of Lamont Sanford in the sitcom *Sanford and Son*?

594) Who was the producer of the science fiction series *Star Trek*?

595) Who was Skip Johnson's wife in the adventure series *Rescue 8*?

596) What actor portrayed Bret Maverick in the western *Maverick*?

597) What police department precinct was depicted in the series *N.Y.P.D.*?
   a. 24th
   b. 25th
   c. 26th
   c. 27th

. . . Answers

586. General Foods

587. Dr. Ann MacGregor

588. *Sergeant Preston of the Yukon*

589. *Broken Arrow*

590. Scott Brady

591. Days, *Life With Father*

592. Shotgun Gibbs

593. Desmond Wilson

594. Gene Roddenberry

595. Patty

596. James Garner

597. d

QUESTIONS

598) What character in the western *Gunsmoke* "brewed a mean pot of coffee"?

599) What is the name of the frustrated pig of the Bugs Bunny cartoons?

600) What sitcom character liked the word "Shazam"?

601) Who was the Notre Dame coach who appeared in the sports feature on *The Ray Anthony Show*?

602) Orphaned Kwai Chang Caine was raised by the monks of what Chinese temple in the western *Kung Fu*?

603) What actor portrayed Napoleon Solo in the spy series *The Man from U.N.C.L.E.*?

604) Who was Foodini's stooge in the puppet series *Lucky Pup*?

605) In the sitcom *Bewitched*, Samantha Stephens's cousin Serena was portrayed by Sandra Gould. True or False?

606) Bob Keeshan, who is Captain Kangaroo, previously portrayed what red-haired, horn-blowing clown in the *Howdy Doody* series?

607) Who was the innkeeper in the western *Cimarron Strip*?

608) What neighbor of Mary Richards was an interior decorator for a local department store in the sitcom *The Mary Tyler Moore Show*?

609) Who was Gillmore Cobb's snobbish wife in the sitcom *My Favorite Husband*?

. . . Answers

598. Chester Goode

599. Elmer T. Fudd

600. Gomer Pyle, *Gomer Pyle, USMC*

601. Frank Leahy

602. Shaolin Temple

603. Robert Vaughn

604. Pinhead

605. False, Serena was played by Elizabeth Montgomery

606. Clarabell

607. Dulcey Coopersmith

608. Rhoda Morgenstern

609. Myra Cobb

610) What do the initials SHADO stand for in the science fiction series *UFO*?

611) What actress hosted *Fireside Theatre* from 1955 to 1958?

612) Who was Sam Jones's first housekeeper in the sitcom *Mayberry R.F.D.*?

613) What two successful situation comedies originated from *All in the Family*?

614) Who were the four commandos featured in the war series *Garrison's Gorillas*?

615) What was the name of Major Gregory "Pappy" Boyington's dog in the war series *Baa Baa Black Sheep*?

616) Arthur Godfrey, Durward Kirby, and Bess Myerson were at various times co-hosts of what humorous series which aired intermittently for 30 years.

617) Who were the three writers of the "Alan Brady Show" in the sitcom *The Dick Van Dyke Show*?

618) Who was the elderly and toothless inmate in the sitcom *On the Rocks*?
   a. Gabby
   b. Shabby
   c. Flabby
   d. Crabby

619) What singer-pianist of *The Lawrence Welk Show* appeared as Santa Claus in the annual Christmas show?

620) Whom did Diane Walker replace as Steve Wilson's romantic interest in the newspaper series *Big Town*?

. . . *Answers*

610. Supreme Headquarters, Alien Defense Organization

611. Jane Wyman

612. Aunt Bea

613. *Maude* and *The Jeffersons*

614. Actor, Casino, Goniff, and Chief

615. Meatball

616. *Candid Camera*

617. Buddy Sorrell, Sally Rogers, and Rob Petrie

618. a

619. Larry Hooper

620. Lorelei Kilbourne

621) Who was Dr. Sam Rinehart's young partner in the medical series *Noah's Ark*?

622) Who was the forest ranger who became Lassie's companion in the adventure series *Lassie*?

623) Nurse Nancy, one of "Pappy's Lambs," was played by Robert Conrad's daughter in the war series *Black Sheep Squadron*. True or False?

624) Who battled the villainous Dr. Fu Manchu in *The Adventures of Fu Manchu*?

625) Who was the widowed owner of the Shady Rest Hotel in the sitcom *Petticoat Junction*?

626) What actor portrayed Jeff Stone in the sitcom *The Donna Reed Show*?

627) Who was the Mexican farmhand in the sitcom *The Real McCoys*?

628) What was the name of the conniving salesman in the sitcom *Green Acres*?

629) Jonathan Rebel was a hand puppet which was featured on what musical variety show of the early 1970's?

630) What did John Boy want to become in the drama series *The Waltons*?
    a. carpenter
    b. novelist
    c. doctor
    d. lawyer

631) Who was the ex-jockey who helped train King in the adventure series *National Velvet*?

. . . Answers

621. Dr. Noah McCann

622. Corey Stuart

623. True, Nancy Conrad

624. Sir Dennis Nayland-Smith

625. Kate Bradley

626. Paul Petersen

627. Pepino

628. Mr. Haney

629. *The Bobby Goldsboro Show*

630. b

631. Mi Taylor

632) Who was the aspiring actor and cab driver in the sitcom *Taxi*?

633) What was the name of the agent who made occasional appearances on the *I Love Lucy* shows?

634) What quiz show of the late 1970's was hosted by Jack Clark and featured a "Cross-fire" finale?

635) Who was the owner of the Scalplock General Store in the western *The Iron Horse*?

636) What "cool" sitcom character liked the word "nerd"?

637) What was the name of the father-and-son law firm in the courtoom series *The Defenders*?

638) What was the name of the Jetsons' family robot in the cartoon series *The Jetsons*?
   a. Jeannie
   b. Elsie
   c. Elroy
   d. Rosey

639) Who was the head nurse in the medical series *Medical Center*?

640) In *The Jackie Gleason Show: The American Scene Magazine* who portrayed Crazy Guggenheim?

641) How many freckles did Howdy Doody have on his face, the amount equaling the number of states in the United States at the time in the 1950's?
   a. 47
   b. 48
   c. 49
   d. 50

. . . *Answers*

632. Bobby Wheeler

633. Jerry

634. *The Cross-Wits*

635. Julie Parsons

636. Fonzie, *Happy Days*

637. Preston & Preston

638. d

639. Nurse Wilcox

640. Frank Fontaine

641. b

642) What relation was Granny to Jed Clampett in the sitcom *The Beverly Hillbillies*?

643) What do the initials SCPD stand for in the police series *The Rookies*?

644) What actress portrayed the telephone operator whose memorable lines included: "one ringy-dingy, two ringy-dingies . . ." in *Rowan & Martin's Laugh-In*?

645) The science fiction series *Star Trek* was set in the 24th century. True or False?

646) What actor portrayed the English corporal Peter Newkirk in the sitcom *Hogan's Heroes*?

647) What was the name of the bartender in the sitcom *Flo*?

648) What was the number of Maxwell Smart's apartment in the sitcom *Get Smart*?

649) "I Am Woman" was the theme song of what musical variety series which was aired during the summer of 1973?

650) What was Gwent in the science fiction series *Space: 1999*?

651) What sitcom character is noted for the exclamation: "I know nothing!"?

652) Who were the Erwins' two children in the sitcom *The Stu Erwin Show*?

653) What singing group was featured on the music show *Rollin' on the River*?

. . . Answers

642. Mother-in-law

643. Southern California Police Department

644. Lily Tomlin

645. False, 23rd century

646. Richard Dawson

647. Earl

648. 86

649. *The Helen Reddy Show*

650. A man-turned-machine

651. Sgt. Hans Schultz, *Hogan's Heroes*

652. Joyce and Jackie

653. Kenny Rogers and the First Edition

654) What character did Goldie Hawn portray in the sitcom *Good Morning, World*?

655) Who was the beautiful French switchboard operator in the detective series *77 Sunset Strip*?

656) At what fort was F Troop stationed in the sitcom with the same name?
    a. Fort Hope
    b. Fort Courage
    c. Fort Trust
    d. Fort Fortitude

657) What character did Brad Johnson portray in the western *Annie Oakley*?

658) To where was Steve Douglas transferred at the start of the 1967 season in the sitcom *My Three Sons*?

659) Who was Sgt. Ernie Bilko's commanding officer in the sitcom *The Phil Silvers Show: You'll Never Get Rich*?

660) What actress portrayed the role of Clementine Hale in the western *Alias Smith and Jones*?

661) Who was the Venusian in the children's series *Tom Corbett, Space Cadet*?

662) Who played Frank Serpico in the police series *Serpico*?

663) Capt. Amos Burke left his job as a Los Angeles chief of detectives to become a secret agent during the final season of *Burke's Law*. True or False?

664) What office did Col. Steve Austin work for after becoming "the Six Million Dollar Man" in the series with the same name?

. . . Answers

654. Sandy Kramer

655. Suzanne Fabray

656. b

657. Deputy Sheriff Lofty Craig

658. North Hollywood, California

659. Col. John Hall

660. Sally Field

661. Astro

662. David Birney

663. True

664. Office of Scientific Information

665) Whom did Mary Ingalls marry in the drama series *Little House on the Prairie*?

666) What character did Denver Pyle portray in the adventure series *The Life and Times of Grizzly Adams*?

667) On what talk show of the late 1970's was Avery Schreiber the resident comedian?

668) In what career was Ann Marie of the sitcom *That Girl*?

669) From which of the following belongings of the Lone Ranger's dead brother was the hero's mask made in the western *The Lone Ranger*?
   a. vest
   b. saddle bags
   c. chaps
   d. hat

670) What was the name of Elizabeth Reynolds's younger brother in the western *The Road West*?

671) Lt. Cdr. Quinton McHale was the commander of PT Boat 53 in the sitcom *McHale's Navy*. True or False?

672) What was the longest running lawyer series?

673) What was the name of Fonzie's former girlfriend who rode a motorcycle in the sitcom *Happy Days*?

674) Baba Looey was what cartoon character's sidekick?

675) What was Gidget's word for good-bye in the sitcom *Gidget*?

676) What country western singer sang the theme "The Ballad of Johnny Yuma" in the western *The Rebel*?

. . . *Answers*

665. Adam Kendall

666. Mad Jack

667. *Sammy and Company*

668. Acting

669. a

670. Chance

671. False, PT Boat 73

672. *Perry Mason*

673. Pinky Tuscadero

674. Quick Draw McGraw

675. "Toodles"

676. Johnny Cash

677) What was the name of the orphaned boy who became Lassie's second companion in the adventure series *Lassie*?

678) Who was the resident priest in the sitcom *M*A*S*H*?

679) What actor portrayed Lucy Carmichael's friend Harry in the sitcom *The Lucy Show*?

680) The Harry Zimmerman Orchestra and later The Peter Matz Orchestra were regulars in what comedy variety series which aired for more than ten years, the final telecast being aired on September 8, 1979?

681) What was the name of Ralph Kramden's and Ed Norton's bowling team in the sitcom *The Honeymooners*?
   a. Hurricanes
   b. Tornadoes
   c. Twisters
   d. Windbreakers

682) Mickey Braddock, star of the adventure series *Circus Boy* from 1956 to 1958, was also Mickey of the sitcom *The Monkees*. True or False?

683) What character called his mother "Mumsie" in the sitcom *The Many Loves of Dobie Gillis*?

684) Who was the McLaughlins' ranch hand in the adventure series *My Friend Flicka*?

685) What war drama was based on the 918th Bombardment Group of the U.S. Eighth Air Force?

686) What was the name of Jim Briggs's father in the police series *Felony Squad*?

. . . Answers

677. Timmy

678. Father John Mulcahy

679. Dick Martin

680. *The Carol Burnett Show*

681. a

682. True, his real last name is Dolenz and he used it in 1966

683. Chatsworth Osborne, Jr.

684. Gus

685. *Twelve O'Clock High*

686. Desk Sgt. Dan Briggs

687) Who was "the silver fox" in the sitcom *The Mary Tyler Moore Show*?

688) How did Andy attract a criminal in the sitcom *The Andy Griffith Show*?

689) The lives of what three criminals were presented in *The Gangster Chronicles*?

690) What was the name of Tony Baretta's cockatoo in the police series *Baretta*?

691) What was the name of the mini-series which featured an Irishman whose dream was to have one of his sons become the first Irish Catholic president?

692) What actor portrayed Deputy U.S. Marshal Sam Buckhart in the western *Law of the Plainsman*?

693) Who was the gym teacher at Mrs. Nestor's Private School in the sitcom *Our Miss Brooks*?

694) What character in the sitcom *Barney Miller* found happiness in coffee making?

695) Who was Peter Christopher's occasional wife in the sitcom *Occasional Wife*?

696) What was the name of the jazz night club which Kaz frequented in the lawyer series *Kaz*?
    a. Meeting Place
    b. Market Place
    c. Starting Gate
    d. Finish Line

697) During the five-year run of the sitcom *Bachelor Father*, how many secretaries did Bentley Gregg employ?

. . . Answers

687. Ted Baxter

688. The aroma of a pie cooling on a windowsill

689. Lucky Luciano, Bugsy Siegel, and Michael Lasker

690. Fred

691. *Captains and Kings*

692. Michael Ansara

693. Gene Talbot

694. Det. Nick Yemana

695. Greta

696. c

697. Five: Vickie, Kitty Deveraux, Kitty Marsh, Suzanne Collins, and Connie

698) Character John James Audubon was a pirate in the western *The Adventures of Jim Bowie*. True or False?

699) Sock and Mandy were never married in the sitcom *The People's Choice*. True or False?

700) What were the June Taylor Dancers of *The Ed Sullivan Show* formerly called?

701) In what game show emceed by Bill Cullen did four contestants try to guess the retail price of merchandise prizes?

702) Who was Rhoda's boyfriend and future husband in the sitcom *Rhoda*?

703) Besides *Green Acres*, what other sitcom of the late 1960's was set in the town of Hooterville?

704) Who did Bob's secretary Carol marry in the sitcom *The Bob Newhart Show*?

705) Who was WKRP's news director in the sitcom *WKRP in Cincinnati*?

706) What was the name of Jerry North's wife in the comedy series *Mr. & Mrs. North*?
   a. Fay
   b. Jamie
   c. Lee
   d. Pamela

707) Who was the Earl of Greystoke in the adventure series *Tarzan*?

708) What actor portrayed Habib, Jeannie II's master, in the sitcom *I Dream of Jeannie*?

. . . Answers

698. False, a painter

699. False

700. the Toastettes

701. *The Price is Right*

702. Joe Gerard

703. *Petticoat Junction*

704. Larry Bondurant

705. Les Nessman

706. d

707. Tarzan

708. Ted Cassidy

709) What was the name of Christopher Colt's cousin in the series *Colt .45*?

710) Who was Diana's neurotic brother in the sitcom *I'm a Big Girl Now*?

711) What talk show host often exclaimed "Marvelous! Smashing! Terrific! It's been a joy having you here!"?

712) Who was Stewart MacMillan's first assistant who later was promoted to lieutenant in the police series *MacMillan and Wife*?

713) What was the name of Festus Haggen's mule in western *Gunsmoke*?
   a. Ruth
   b. Hilda
   c. Packy
   d. Pauline

714) Who replaced Freddie as Joey Barnes's manager in the sitcom *The Joey Bishop Show*?

715) What controversial folk singer caused problems for CBS with his Vietnam protest song entitled "Knee Deep in the Big Muddy" performed on *The Smothers Brothers Comedy Hour*?

716) What was the name of the president of the bus company in the sitcom *The Honeymooners*?

717) Who was the lieutenant intent on recapturing Dr. Richard Kimble in *The Fugitive*?

718) What actor portrayed Billy Jim Hawkins in the lawyer series *Hawkins*?

719) Who was the tennis pro murdered on the sitcom *Soap*?

. . . Answers

709. Sam Colt, Jr.

710. Walter Douglass

711. David Frost

712. Sgt. Charles Enright

713. a

714. Larry Corbett

715. Pete Seeger

716. Mr. Monahan

717. Lt. Philip Gerard

718. James Stewart

719. Peter Campbell

720) "Book 'Em" were the closing words of what lead character in what series?

721) Which of the following outlaws was not killed in the famous shootout at the O.K. Corral in the western *The Life and Legend of Wyatt Earp*?
   a. Frank McLaury
   b. Tom McLaury
   c. Billy Clanton
   d. Ike Clanton

722) Who was Stu Erwin's wife in the sitcom *The Stu Erwin Show*?

723) Who was the only married member of the trio featured in the police series *The Rookies*?

724) What actor portrayed Father Chuck O'Malley in the sitcom *Going My Way*?

725) "So You Want to Lead a Band" was a popular routine featured on what musical variety show of the 1950's?

726) What was the featured couple's last name in the sitcom *Ethel and Albert*?

727) Mike Andros was an investigative reporter for the *New York Herald* in the newspaper series *The Andros Targets*. True or False?

728) What type of car did Dave Crabtree purchase in the sitcom *My Mother the Car*?

729) What actress portrayed Ann Morrison, Albie's teenaged daughter, in the sitcom *The Pride of the Family*?

730) What was the previous title of *The Alfred Hitchcock Hour*?

. . . Answers

720. Steve McGarrett, *Hawaii Five-O*

721. d

722. June

723. Mike Danko

724. Gene Kelly

725. *The Sammy Kaye Show*

726. Arbuckle

727. False, *The New York Forum*

728. 1928 Porter

729. Natalie Wood

730. *Alfred Hitchcock Presents*

QUESTIONS

731) "It's All Relative" and "What Is It?" were two features of what variety show which often dealt with controversial issues?

732) What musician is known for the "Theme from Shaft" in the detective series *Shaft*?

733) In "Peabody's Improbable History," a feature of *The Bullwinkle Show*, who was Peabody's adopted boy companion?

734) What U.S. Navy ship was used for the filming of *The Silent Service* series?

735) What actor, who played a farmer known as Mr. Edwards in the series *Little House on the Prairie*, left the show and got his own series, *Carter Country*?

736) What high school did Judy Jetson attend in the cartoon series *The Jetsons*?
   a. Galaxy High School
   b. Meteorite High School
   c. Solar High School
   d. Orbit High School

737) What sitcom family lived at 211 Pine Street in Mayfield, USA?

738) What actor portrayed Father Samuel Cavanaugh in the drama series *Sarge*?

739) What was the name of the police lieutenant portrayed by Mike Road in series *The Roaring Twenties*?

740) Emmet Clark was the fix-it-shop owner in the sitcom *Mayberry, R.F.D.* True or False?

741) Who did Anson Williams portray in the sitcom *Happy Days*?

. . . Answers

731. *The Jack Paar Show*

732. Isaac Hayes

733. Sherman

734. *U.S.S. Sawfish*

735. Victor French

736. d

737. Cleavers, *Leave it to Beaver*

738. George Kennedy

739. Lt. Joe Switolski

740. True

741. Warren "Potsie" Weber

742) What is the name of the two cartoon chipmunks of the Walt Disney cartoons?

743) What was the name of the spirit who inhabited the cottage in the sitcom *The Ghost and Mrs. Muir*?

744) What Red Skelton character was noted for the phrase "I dood it!" in the comedy variety series *The Red Skelton Show*?

745) Who were the two younger rangers featured in the western *Laredo*?

746) What was the name of the Hansens' dog in the comedy series *Mama*?
    a. Willie   c. Billie
    b. Millie   d. Tillie

747) What character did Billy Mumy portray in the science fiction series *Lost in Space*?

748) What sitcom of the late 1970's was set in the small town of Clinton Corners?

749) What actor portrayed Fred Mertz in the *I Love Lucy* show?

750) What was the name of Pancho's horse in the western *The Cisco Kid*?

751) During the five-year run of the detective series *Martin Kane, Private Eye,* how many actors portrayed Martin Kane?
    a. one   c. three
    b. two   d. four

752) What was the name of the Munsters' pet bat in the sitcom *The Munsters*?

. . . Answers

742. Chip 'n' Dale

743. Captain Daniel Gregg

744. The Mean Widdle Kid

745. Chad Cooper and Joe Riley

746. a

747. Will Robinson

748. *Carter Country*

749. William Frawley

750. Loco

751. d

752. Igor

753) George and Marion Kerby, along with their St. Bernard, died in a boating accident during a European vacation in the sitcom *Topper*. True or False?

754) Who was Barth Gimble's sidekick in the *Fernwood 2-Night* series?

755) "Back in the Saddle Again" was the theme song of what western of the early 1950's?

756) Who replaced Inspector Shiller as Tony Baretta's boss in the police series *Baretta*?

757) What types of animals were Calvin and the Colonel in the cartoon series with same name?

758) What character did James Gregory portray in the police series *The Lawless Years*?

759) What was the name of Owen Marshall's daughter in the law series *Owen Marshall, Counselor at Law*?

760) What actress portrayed Audra Barkley in the western *The Big Valley*?

761) What sitcom "couple" lived at 1049 Park Avenue in Manhattan?

762) What character did Lloyd Nolan portray in the sitcom *Julia*?

763) *The Men* was the umbrella title for what three adventure series?

. . . Answers

753. False, they died in an avalanche

754. Jerry Hubbard

755. *The Gene Autry Show*

756. Lt. Hal Brubaker

757. Bear and fox, respectively

758. Barney Ruditsky

759. Melissa

760. Linda Evans

761. Felix Unger and Oscar Madison, *The Odd Couple*

762. Dr. Morton Chegley

763. *Assignment Vienna, Delphi Bureau,* and *Jigsaw*

764) From which war was Capt. Adam Troy a veteran in the *Adventures of Paradise* series?

    a. War of 1812   c. World War I

    b. Civil War   d. Korean War

765) What actor portrayed Perry Mason in the lawyer series with the same name?

766) Who was Doris Martin's boss and editor of *Today's World* magazine in the sitcom *The Doris Day Show*?

767) What do the initials J.J. stand for in the sitcom title *The Governor & J.J.*?

768) Who was Slate Shannon's female companion in the adventure series *Bold Venture*?

769) What was the name of the soda shop's overweight waitress in the sitcom *What's Happening*?

770) What did Cpl. Maxwell Klinger's baseball shirt have printed on it in the *M*A*S*H* series?

771) Cathedral General Hospital was the hospital featured in the sitcom *Temperatures Rising*. True or False?

772) What was the name of the oldest Macahan offspring in the western *How the West Was Won*?

    a. Luke   c. Josh

    b. Laura   d. Jessie

773) What character did Dick Peabody portray in the war series *Combat*?

774) What was the name of the architect in the science fiction series *The Invaders* who sought to inform the world of alien creatures?

. . . Answers

764. d

765. Raymond Burr

766. Michael Nicholson

767. Jennifer Jo

768. Sailor Duval

769. Shirley

770. Mud Hens

771. False, Capital General Hospital

772. a

773. Littlejohn

774. David Vincent

775) What character did Debbie Reynolds portray in the sitcom *The Debbie Reynolds Show*?

776) Who was chief of staff of the hospital complex in the medical series *Medical Center*?

777) Which of the following actors did not portray the bartender Sam O'Brien in the western *Gunsmoke*?
   a. Brian Keith   c. Clem Fuller
   b. Glenn Strange   d. Robert Brubaker

778) "Melancholy Serenade" was the theme song of what popular comedy variety series?

779) Who was the affectionate dog in the *Soupy Sales* children's show?

780) What actor portrayed Glenn Evans in the adventure series *Hong Kong*?

781) Hymie was the name of CONTROL's robot in the sitcom *Get Smart*. True or False?

782) What was the name of the sitcom which featured sitcom spouses who were also married in real life and in which the husband was a cartoonist?

783) What was the name of the Queen of Astheria in the science fiction series *Space: 1999*?

784) How much money did Ed Norton and Ralph Kramden earn per week in the sitcom *The Honeymooners*?

785) What was the name of the hospital in which Robert Ironside convalesced in the *Ironside* series?
   a. St. Catharine's Hospital   c. St. Joan's Hospital
   b. St. Ann's Hospital   d. St. Mary's Hospital

. . . *Answers*

775. Debbie Thompson

776. Dr. Paul Lochner

777. a

778. *The Jackie Gleason Show*

779. Black Tooth

780. Rod Taylor

781. True

782. *He & She*

783. Arra

784. $62.00

785. d

786) What was the name of Huggy Bear's bar in the police series *Starsky and Hutch*?

787) What was Toby called as a boy in the drama series *Roots*?

788) What was the theme song in the sitcom *Gilligan's Island*?

789) Who was Sen. Hayes Stowe's administrative assistant in the political series *The Senator*?

790) *Ensign O'Toole* was set in an intense period of World War II conflict. True or False?

791) What was the name of Annie Oakley's brother in the western *Annie Oakley*?

792) What sitcom featured a father and daughter who lived at the Carlton Arms Apartment Building located on East 57th Street in New York?

793) Who was Martin Peyton's murdered bride-to-be in the soap *Peyton Place*?

794) What was the name of the forest in *The Adventures of Robin Hood* series?

795) What type of dog was Asta in the detective series *The Thin Man*?
   a. fox terrier   c. bloodhound
   b. sheep dog   d. German Shepherd

796) How many members belonged to the group Sha Na Na in the musical variety show with the same name?

797) Who was the base commander in the sitcom *Broadside*?

798) How was Col. Steve Austin originally injured in the adventure series *The Six Million Dollar Man*?

. . . *Answers*

786. The Pits

787. Kunta Kinte

788. "The Ballad of Gilligan's Island"

789. Jordan Boyle

790. False, it was set in peacetime

791. Tagg Oakley

792. *My Little Margie*

793. Adrienne Van Leyden

794. Sherwood Forest

795. a

796. Ten

797. Cdr. Rogers Adrian

798. The moon-landing craft crashed in a test over the desert

799) Who was the owner of the general store in the series *Little House on the Prairie*?

800) What actress portrayed June Cleaver in the sitcom *Leave it to Beaver*?

801) What was the name of Fred Sanford's deceased wife in the sitcom *Sanford and Son*?

802) What character did Barry Sullivan portray in the series *The Road West*?

803) Hounddog, Apocalypse, and Oblivion were all frontier towns featured in the western *Maverick*. True or False?

804) Where was the Guestward Ho Ranch located in the sitcom *Guestward Ho!*?
   a. Nevada
   b. Colorado
   c. New Mexico
   d. Arizona

805) What actress portrayed Kitty Russell in the western *Gunsmoke*?

806) What was the theme song of the sitcom *Laverne & Shirley*?

807) With what department was Prof. Ray McNutley associated in the series *Meet Mr. McNutley*?

808) What was the name of the international crime syndicate in the spy series *The Man from U.N.C.L.E.*?

809) Lucas was never married in the drama series *Lucas Tanner*. True or False?

810) What actor portrayed Chief Roy Mobey in the sitcom *Carter Country*?

. . . *Answers*

799. Nels Oleson

800. Barbara Billingsley

801. Elizabeth

802. Benjamin Pride

803. True

804. c

805. Amanda Blake

806. "Making Our Dreams Come True"

807. English

808. THRUSH

809. False, his wife and son died in a car accident

810. Victor French

811) What was the name of Zeb's brother in the series *How the West Was Won?*

812) Who was the former Oxford criminology professor who aided in case analysis in the detective series *Checkmate?*

813) Who did Dr. Steven Kiley marry in the medical series *Marcus Welby, M.D.?*

814) Where in Mindy's apartment were Mork's sleeping quarters located in the sitcom *Mork & Mindy?*
    a. closet   c. attic
    b. basement   d. ceiling

815) What captain from *M*A*S*H* was featured in his own series?

816) What actress portrayed Sister Bertrille in the sitcom *The Flying Nun?*

817) What was the name of Dr. Richard Kimble's sister in *The Fugitive?*

818) What were the names of the Dragons' two bulldogs in the musical variety series *The Captain and Tennille?*

819) What Champagne Lady was fired in 1959 because she showed "too much knee" on *The Lawrence Welk Show?*

820) Who were the two detectives featured in the sitcom *The Partners?*

821) What actor portrayed Bat Masterson in the western with the same name?

. . . Answers

811. Timothy

812. Carl Hyatt

813. Janet Blake

814. c

815. Capt. John McIntyre, *Trapper John, M.D.*

816. Sally Field

817. Donna Taft

818. Elizabeth and Broderick

819. Alice Lon

820. Lennie Crooke and George Robinson

821. Gene Barry

822) What newspaper did Oscar Madison write for in the sitcom *The Odd Couple*?

    a. *New York Tribune*   c. *New York News*

    b. *New York Herald*   d. *New York Today*

823) Who was the ranch handyman in the comedy series *Kentucky Jones*?

824) What was the name of Corie Bratter's mother in the sitcom *Barefoot in the Park*?

825) Mr. Fields ran an acting school in *The Abbott and Costello Show*. True or False?

826) "You are never far away from me" was part of the closing theme of what musical variety show of the late 1950's and early 1960's?

827) What was the squadron number of *Emergency's* Paramedical Rescue Service?

    a. 31   c. 51

    b. 41   d. 61

828) What was the name of Britt Reid's faithful manservant in the crime series *The Green Hornet*?

829) What character did Joi Lansing portray in the sitcom *Love That Bob*?

830) Who were the two featured disc jockeys in the sitcom *WKRP in Cincinnati*?

831) Who was Dick Preston's manager during the time he was a local talk show host in the sitcom *The New Dick Van Dyke Show*?

. . . Answers

822. b

823. Seldom Jackson

824. Mabel Bates

825. False, a boardinghouse

826. *The Perry Como Show*

827. c

828. Kato

829. Shirley Swanson

830. Dr. Johnny Fever and Venus Flytrap

831. Bernie Davis

QUESTIONS

832) The *Enterprise's* captain won the boat in a poker game in the adventure series *Riverboat*. True or False?

833) What was the name of Herbert Philbrick's wife in the intrigue series *I Led Three Lives*?

834) What was Lieutenant Columbo's first name in the police series *Columbo*?
    a. Frank   c. Robert
    b. Peter   d. none of these

835) What character did Edward Binns portray in the intrigue series *It Takes a Thief*?

836) Who was Lily's accomplice in the sitcom *December Bride*?

837) What actor portrayed Commissioner Stewart MacMillan in the police series *MacMillan and Wife*?

838) What was the name of the pediatrician in the sitcom *The Joey Bishop Show*?

839) What type of animal did Honey West have for a pet in the detective series *Honey West*?
    a. ocelot   c. chimpanzee
    b. fox   d. tarantula

840) Maxwell Smart was also known under what agent number in the sitcom *Get Smart*?

841) Who was the naval dentist in the comedy series *Hennessey*?

842) Who was the nutty socialite whose yacht was anchored beside the detectives' houseboat in the *Surfside Six* series?

. . . Answers

832. True

833. Eva Philbrick

834. d (he didn't have a first name)

835. Wallie Powers

836. Hilda Crocker

837. Rock Hudson

838. Dr. Sam Nolan

839. a

840. Agent 86

841. Harvey Spencer Blair III

842. Daphne Dutton

QUESTIONS

843) Who was Pete Dixon's girlfriend in the drama series *Room 222*?

844) What sitcom family lived at 1030 East Tremont Avenue in the Bronx?

845) How did Kookie describe a bad week in the detective series *77 Sunset Strip*?

846) What were the names of the orphaned twins in the sitcom *Family Affair*?

847) The character Lillian Nuvo was portrayed by Sue Ann Langdon in the sitcom *Arnie*. True or False?

848) Who assumed the role of newscaster after Chevy Chase left *NBC's Saturday Night Live*?

849) To whom did the vice-squad team report in the police series *Police Woman*?

850) In what form did Tom Smothers return to earth in the sitcom *The Smothers Brothers Show*?
    a. superhero   c. reincarnated clone
    b. angel   d. ghost

851) What quiz show featured three contestants who all claimed to be the same individual?

852) What actor portrayed John Shaft in the detective series *Shaft*?

853) In "Adventures of Dudley Doright," a feature of *The Bullwinkle Show*, what was the name of the evil character?

854) What company sponsored the musical variety show *Shower of Stars*?

. . . Answers

843. Liz McIntyre

844. The Goldbergs, *The Goldbergs*

845. "A dark seven"

846. Buffy and Jody

847. True

848. Jane Curtin

849. Lt. Bill Crowley

850. b

851. *To Tell the Truth*

852. Richard Roundtree

853. Snidely Whiplash

854. Chrysler Corporation

855) Who was Chester Riley's neighbor and best friend in the sitcom *The Life of Riley*?

856) Ward Cleaver was an engineer in the sitcom *Leave it to Beaver*. True or False?

857) What was the name of the show which featured members of "The Probe Division of World Securities"?

858) Who was Sam McCloud's romantic interest in the police series *McCloud*?

859) Who was the town drunk in the western *Gunsmoke*?
    a. Louie   c. Hank
    b. Percy   d. Barney

860) Lassie was portrayed as a male collie in the adventure series *Lassie*. True or False?

861) What character replaced Maj. Frank Burns in the sitcom *M*A*S*H*?

862) Who was Stanley Belmont's unemployed brother-in-law in the sitcom *Lotsa Luck*?

863) Who was Carol Burnett's co-star during the first ten years of the comedy-variety series *The Carol Burnett Show*?

864) Who sponsored the *I Love Lucy* shows?

865) What type of animal was Bimbo, Corky's pet in the adventure series *Circus Boy*?
    a. chimpanzee   c. snake
    b. rabbit   d. elephant

866) Who was held hostage by a mass murderer in the soap *Mary Hartman, Mary Hartman*?

. . . Answers

855. Jim Gillis

856. False, an accountant

857. *Search*

858. Chris Coughlin

859. a

860. False, Lassie was portrayed as a female although all the collies who portrayed Lassie were male.

861. Maj. Charles Emerson Winchester

862. Arthur Swann

863. Harvey Korman

864. Philip Morris

865. d

866. Heather Hartman, Mary's daughter

867) Moose and Mickey were the two truckers who made occasional appearances in the adventure series *Movin' On*. True or False?

868) What was Kathy Anderson's nickname in the sitcom *Father Knows Best*?

869) By what other title was the sitcom *Oh! Susanna* known?

870) What were the names of the two officers assigned to Car 54 in the sitcom *Car 54, Where Are You*?

871) What was the first 90-minute Western series?
    a. *Bonanza*
    b. *Gunsmoke*
    c. *The Deputy*
    d. *The Virginian*

872) Who was the marshal under which Sam Buckhart served in the western *Law of the Plainsman*?

873) Who was the "Outsider" in the detective series with the same name?

874) To whom did the late Mr. Strickland leave his inheritance in the sitcom *The Betty Hutton Show*?

875) Who was Will Stockdale's girlfriend in the sitcom *No Time for Sergeants*?

876) In what city was Carl Kolchak a crime reporter in the occult series *Kolchak: The Night Stalker*?
    a. Philadelphia
    b. Chicago
    c. New York
    d. Miami

. . . Answers

867. False, Moose and Benjy

868. Kitten

869. *The Gale Storm Show*

870. Gunther Toody and Francis Muldoon

871. d

872. Marshal Andy Morrison

873. David Ross

874. Goldie Appleby

875. Millie

876. b

877) What was the name of the detective series which had become very popular among Polish-Americans and which was originally aired as a segment of *NBC's Wednesday Mystery Movie*?

878) What was the name of the pirate in the western *The Adventures of Jim Bowie*?

879) Who was Peter Gunn's lieutenant friend in the detective series *Peter Gunn*?

880) What was the name of the hospital which provided its services to the paramedics in the drama series *Emergency*?
  a. Summit   c. Franzen
  b. Rampart   d. Mercer

881) What was the name of Fred Ziffel's pet pig in the sitcom *Green Acres*?

882) What was the title of Bob Cummings's third comedy series?

883) What character was portrayed by Ellen Corby in the drama series *The Waltons*?

884) Who was the nanny in the sitcom *Nanny and the Professor*?

885) How many different casts comprised the *Temperatures Rising* sitcom?
  a. one   c. three
  b. two   d. four

886) What sitcom spouses lived at 623 East 68th Street in Manhattan?

887) What actor portrayed Count Dracula in the series *The Curse of Dracula*?

. . . Answers

877. *Banacek*

878. Jean Lafitte

879. Lieutenant Jacoby

880. b

881. Arnold

882. *The Bob Cummings Show*

883. Esther (Grandma) Walton

884. Phoebe Figalilly

885. c

886. Lucy and Ricky Ricardo, *I Love Lucy*

887. Michael Nouri

888) Dr. Peter Brady worked for the FBI in the intrigue series *The Invisible Man*. True or False?

889) What late night television talk show of the early 1970's featured Bobby Rosengarden as its orchestra leader?

890) Which of the following characters was not a "hippie cop" in the police series *The Mod Squad*?
a. Steve Garrett   c. Linc Hayes
b. Pete Cochran   d. Julie Barnes

891) What actress portrayed hospital administrative assistant Ann Anderson in the sitcom *House Calls*?

892) What was the name of Big John's younger brother in the western *The High Chaparral*?

893) What actress made occasional appearances in her portrayal of Marion, the ex-wife of Larry in the sitcom *Hello, Larry*?

894) Who were the two detectives featured in the series *Switch*?

895) All the members of the S.W.A.T. squad were Vietnam veterans in the police series *S.W.A.T.* True or False?

896) At what camp was Pvt. Gomer Pyle stationed in the sitcom *Gomer Pyle, U.S.M.C.*?
a. Camp Henderson   c. Camp Hamilton
b. Camp Hawthorne   d. Camp Hastings

897) Who was Chester Tate's wife in the sitcom *Soap*?

898) What was the name of the company which dealt in Hekawi souvenirs in the sitcom *F Troop*?

... _Answers_

888. False, British Intelligence

889. _The Dick Cavett Show_

890. a

891. Lynn Redgrave

892. Buck Cannon

893. Shelley Fabares

894. Pete Ryan and Frank McBride

895. True

896. a

897. Jessica

898. O'Rourke Enterprises

899) What sitcom character was a cartoonist for *Manhattanite Magazine*?

900) Who were the father and son doctors featured in the sitcom *The Practice*?

901) What man and wife team hosted the live interview series *All Around the Town*?

902) Who was the editor of *The Epitaph* in the western *Tombstone Territory*?

903) In what state was the town of Buckskin located in the western series *Buckskin*?
    a. Wyoming
    b. Colorado
    c. Montana
    d. South Dakota

904) What musical variety show of the first half of the 1960's featured the theme song "Sing Along"?

905) Who was the fourth daughter born to Charles and Caroline Ingalls in the series *Little House on the Prairie*?

906) What was the name of Beaver's female classmate who sat in the "smart row" and teased him in the sitcom *Leave it to Beaver*?

907) From whom had Bret Maverick received advice in the western *Maverick*?

908) What actress portrayed Joanie Cunningham in the sitcom *Happy Days*?

. . . *Answers*

899. John Monroe, *My World and Welcome to It*

900. Dr. Jules Bedford and Dr. David Bedford

901. Mike Wallace and Buff Cobb

902. Harris Claibourne

903. c

904. *Sing Along with Mitch*

905. Grace

906. Judy Hessler

907. His "pappy"

908. Erin Moran

909) What was puppet Ophelia Oglepuss's occupation in the children's series *Kukla, Fran, & Ollie*?
   a. opera star
   b. waitress
   c. detective
   d. nurse

910) What was the favorite bar of the *M*A*S*H* unit?

911) What was the name of Prof. John Robinson's wife in the science fiction series *Lost in Space*?

912) All of the Cartwright sons in the western *Bonanza* had different mothers. True or False?

913) Who was the mailwoman in the sitcom *Chico and the Man*?
   a. Mandy
   b. Mabel
   c. Myrtle
   d. Mitzy

914) What was Zelda Gilroy's pet name for Dobie in the sitcom *The Many Loves of Dobie Gillis*?

915) Who was Mindy's swinging grandmother in the sitcom *Mork & Mindy*?

916) What was the name of the insurance company which Jim Anderson managed in the sitcom *Father Knows Best*?

917) What was the name of the evil organization masterminded by Siegfried in the sitcom *Get Smart*?

918) What was the most memorable sketch in the comedy variety series *Caesar's Hour*?

. . . Answers

909. a

910. Rosie's Bar

911. Maureen

912. True

913. b

914. Poopsie

915. Cora Hudson

916. General Insurance Company

917. KAOS

918. "The Commuters"

919) Who was the Topper's maid in the sitcom *Topper*?
   a. Karen
   b. Kim
   c. Katie
   d. Kathy

920) Walter Nichols was the oldest partner in the Nichols, Darrell, and Darrell law firm featured in the lawyer series *The Lawyers*. True or False?

921) Who were Marshal Frank Caine's two deputies in the first season of the western *The Outlaws*?

922) What character did Bettye Ackerman portray in the medical series *Ben Casey*?

923) What was the name of the group organized to find the Northwest Passage in the adventure series *Northwest Passage*?

924) On what network was the police series *Kojak* aired?

925) Elvis Presley in 1955 and Buddy Holly in 1956 both failed auditions for what talent show which was last telecast in 1958?

926) Puppet Oky Doky received his strength from eating raisins in the children's series *Oky Doky Ranch*. True or False?

927) What was Napoleon Solo's agent number in the series *The Man from U.N.C.L.E.*?
   a. #7
   b. #9
   c. #11
   d.#13

. . . *Answers*

919. c

920. True

921. Will Forman and Heck Martin

922. Dr. Maggie Graham

923. Rogers' Rangers

924. CBS

925. *Arthur Godfrey's Talent Scouts*

926. False, pills

927. c

928) Who was the long-haired son-in-law in the sitcom *The Paul Lynde Show*?

929) What character did Raymond Massey portray in the medical series *Dr. Kildare*?

930) What sitcom, which starred Whitman Mayo, was a spin-off of *Sanford and Son*?

931) What musical variety series of the late 1970's was hosted by a singer whose hits included "Roses Are Red My Dear" and "Blue on Blue"?

932) What wagonmaster replaced Major Seth Adams in the western *Wagon Train*?

933) What was the name of the Everetts' sheepdog in the sitcom *Nanny and the Professor*?
    a. Hal
    b. Butch
    c. Prudence
    d. Waldo

934) What was the name of Ann Marie's boyfriend in the sitcom *That Girl*?

935) Bruce Boxleitner portrayed Luke Macahan in the western *How the West Was Won*. True or False?

936) Who was the owner of the Copa Club in the sitcom *Make Room for Daddy*?

937) What actor portrayed Robert Major in the sitcom *Ichabod and Me*?

938) "That's Entertainment" was the theme song of *The Danny Thomas Show*. True or False?

. . . Answers

928. Howie Dickerson

929. Dr. Leonard Gillespie

930. *Grady*

931. *The Bobby Vinton Show*

932. Christopher Hale

933. d

934. Donald Hollinger

935. True

936. Charley Helper

937. Robert Sterling

938. False, "Danny Boy"

QUESTIONS

939) Who was Millie's friend and aspiring writer and composer in the sitcom *Meet Millie*?

940) Which of the following persons was not a member of the Jackson Five rock group featured in the musical variety show *The Jacksons*?
    a. Jackie Jackson
    b. Michael Jackson
    c. Brian Jackson
    d. Marlon Jackson

941) Who was the landlord in the sitcom *Hey Landlord*?

942) What comedy series had "Seattle" as its theme song?

943) What inspector replaced Steve Keller in the police series *The Streets of San Francisco*?

944) Who was Toby's daughter in the drama series *Roots*?

945) What was the name of Bert Gramus's wife in the sitcom *The Good Guys*?

946) Who was the maitre d' of Dino's Restaurant in the series *77 Sunset Strip*?
    a. Luigi
    b. Mario
    c. Marco
    d. Francesco

947) Hershey Park was the name of the Douglases' town in which they lived for seven seasons in the sitcom *My Three Sons*. True or False?

948) What sitcom character of the late 1950's had the following serial number: 15042699?

. . . Answers

939. Alfred Prinzmetal

940. c (the other two were Randy and LaToya)

941. Woody Banner

942. *Here Come the Brides*

943. Inspector Dan Robbins

944. Kizzy

945. Claudia

946. b

947. False, Bryant Park

948. Ernest T. Bilko, *The Phil Silvers Show: You'll Never Get Rich*

QUESTIONS

949) What was the name of Henry Aldrich's best friend in the sitcom *The Aldrich Family*?

950) Who were Michael Endicott's three daughters in the sitcom *To Rome with Love*?

951) What character did Jack Palance portray in the detective series *Bronk*?

952) On which novel was the adventure series *The Six Million Dollar Man* based?
   a. *The Bionic Human*
   b. *Cyborg*
   c. *Hiborg*
   d. *The Bionic Man*

953) What actress portrayed Laura Ingalls Wilder in the series *Little House on the Prairie*?

954) Paul Bryan closed down his medical practice in the adventure series *Run for Your Life*. True or False?

955) What was the name of the Kansas town first marshaled by Wyatt Earp in *The Life and Legend of Wyatt Earp*?

956) What actor portrayed Lt. Cdr. Quinton McHale in the sitcom *McHale's Navy*?

957) What was the name of Fonzie's young cousin in the sitcom *Happy Days*?

958) In what year did the Robinsons' spacecraft depart from earth for Alpha Centauri in the science fiction series *Lost in Space*?
   a. 1987
   b. 1997
   c. 2007
   d. 2017

. . . *Answers*

949. Homer Brown

950. Alison, Penny, and Pokey

951. Lt. Alex Bronkov

952. b

953. Melissa Gilbert

954. False, law practice

955. Ellsworth

956. Ernest Borgnine

957. Chachi Arcola

958. b

959) Subsequent to Lt. Col. Henry Blake's discharge, his helicopter was shot down in the sitcom *M*A*S*H*. True or False?

960) "William Tell Overture" was the theme song of what western which was first telecast in the fall of 1949?

961) What was the name of Centennial's unscrupulous family who sought the power and riches of the land in the drama series *Centennial*?
    a. Catlin
    b. Barrymore
    c. Winchester
    d. Wendell

962) What actor portrayed Hadley Chisholm in the western *The Chisholms*?

963) Patrick Porter was the name of Dr. Welby's grandson in the medical series *Marcus Welby, M.D.* True or False?

964) What sitcom character of the mid 1960's said, "Earth's all right for a visit but I wouldn't want to live here"?

965) What was Sister Bertrille's name before she became a nun in the sitcom *The Flying Nun*?

966) What was the name of George and Gracie's son in the sitcom *The George Burns and Gracie Allen Show*?

967) What storekeeper was associated with the vigilante movement in the western *The Californians*?

968) What was the name of Laverne's father in the sitcom *Laverne & Shirley*?

969) Who was the widowed mother and band member in the sitcom *The Partridge Family*?

. . . Answers

959. True

960. *The Lone Ranger*

961. d

962. Robert Preston

963. False, Phil Porter

964. Uncle Martin, *My Favorite Martian*

965. Elsie Ethington

966. Ronnie Burns

967. Jack McGivern

968. Frank DeFazio

969. Shirley Partridge

QUESTIONS

970) How many actresses portrayed Beulah in the sitcom *Beulah*?
    a. one
    b. two
    c. three
    d. four

971) Who was Will Stockdale's sergeant in the sitcom *No Time for Sergeants*?

972) What actor portrayed Clinton Judd in the lawyer series *Judd, For the Defense*?

973) "Till then, to put a little fun in your life, try dancing" was the closing line of what musical variety series of the 1950's?

974) Who replaced Clay Baker as Capt. Adam Troy's first mate in the *Adventures in Paradise* series?

975) Michelle was the name of Tony Petrocelli's wife in the lawyer series *Petrocelli*. True or False?

976) What was the name of the Green Hornet's car in the crime series *The Green Hornet*?
    a. Black Beauty
    b. Betty Bullet
    c. Foil Freddy
    d. Combat Kid

977) What actress portrayed Miss Larson in the sitcom *The Bob Newhart Show*?

978) At what high school was Ken Reeves a basketball coach in the drama series *The White Shadow*?

979) Who was producer of the soap opera "Those Who Care" in the sitcom *The New Dick Van Dyke Show*?

. . . Answers

970. b (Ethel Waters and Louise Beavers)

971. Sergeant King

972. Carl Betz

973. *The Arthur Murray Party*

974. Chris Parker

975. False, Maggie

976. a

977. Penny Marshall

978. Carver High School

979. Max Mathias

980) Who was referred to as "Slick" in the detective series *Vegas*?

981) "Frat Mers" was the way Desi Arnaz pronounced what character's name in the *I Love Lucy* shows?

982) What was the name of the Tracys' pet chimpanzee in the adventure series *Daktari*?
   a. Judy
   b. Bethie
   c. Hillary
   d. Jamie

983) Sonny Mann was a violinist in the sitcom *It's a Living*. True or False?

984) Four of the dancing Golddiggers later became the Ding-a-Ling Sisters in *The Dean Martin Show*. True or False?

985) What type of vehicle appeared in the first season of the police series *The Mod Squad*?

986) What was the name of Joe and Katie Wabashes' daughter in the sitcom *Joe's World*?

987) What sitcom character's social security number is is 105-36-22?

988) "Only a Man" was the theme song of what drama series which starred Andy Griffith?

989) Which member of the "Rat Patrol" was an Englishman in the war series with the same name?
   a. Pvt. Mark Hitchcock
   b. Sgt. Sam Troy
   c. Sgt. Jack Moffitt
   d. Pvt. Tully Pettigrew

. . . Answers

980. Philip Roth

981. Fred Mertz

982. a

983. False, a piano player

984. True

985. A "Woody"

986. Maggie

987. Ralph Kramden, *The Honeymooners*

988. *The Headmaster*

989. c

990) In what hotel was the Boom Boom Room located in the *Surfside Six* series?

991) A line from the 1969 Creedence Clearwater Revival hit "Proud Mary" was used as the title of what music show of the early 1970's?

992) What actress portrayed Ginger in the sitcom *Gilligan's Island*?

993) Who were the Tates' three children in the sitcom *Soap*?

994) What was the name of the U.S. destroyer featured in the sitcom *Ensign O'Toole*?
   a. *Pacer*   c. *Appleby*
   b. *Peach Bottom*   d. *Trojan*

995) What did Bob McDonald name the robot that was left in his care in the sitcom *My Living Doll*?

996) Who were the "protectors" in the adventure series with the same name?

997) Nick Charles was a retired drill sergeant in the comedy series *The Thin Man*. True or False?

998) What actor portrayed Det. Tim Tilson in the police series *Burke's Law*?

999) What was unique about the supporting actors in the western *Shotgun Slade*?

1000) What sitcom family lived at 1313 Blue View Terrace in Los Angeles?

1001) What actor portrayed Wyatt Earp in the western *The Life and Legend of Wyatt Earp*?

. . . Answers

990. Fontainebleau Hotel

991. *Rollin' on the River*

992. Tina Louise

993. Corrine, Eunice, and Billy

994. c

995. Rhoda

996. Harry Rule, Contessa di Contini, and Paul Buchet

997. False, a retired detective

998. Gary Conway

999. They were well-known personalities from various fields such as sports, military, and music.

1000. The Rileys, *The Life of Riley*

1001. Hugh O'Brien

1002) Fonzie never received his high school diploma in the sitcom *Happy Days*. True or False?

1003) What was the name of Lucy Carmichael's divorced friend in the sitcom *The Lucy Show*?
    a. Vivian Bagley   c. Gail Bagley
    b. Mary Jane Bagley   d. Polly Bagley

1004) What character did Tim Conway portray in the sitcom *McHale's Navy*?

1005) What was the name of the sheriff in the western *Laramie*?

1006) What do the initials U.N.C.L.E. stand for in the spy series *The Man from U.N.C.L.E.*?

1007) Chico was cast as a Vietnam veteran in the sitcom *Chico and the Man*. True or False?

1008) What actor portrayed Joe Mannix in the detective series *Mannix*?

1009) What was the name of the dolphin who played Flipper in the adventure series *Flipper*?
    a. Lizzy   c. Sandy
    b. Suzy   d. Candy

1010) What was the name of the mailman in the sitcom *The George Burns and Gracie Allen Show*?

1011) Who was Captain Video's sidekick in the children's series *Captain Video and His Video Rangers*?

1012) "I Love You Truly" was one of the viewers' favorite songs featured in what music series which ran for 16 years on ABC?

. . . Answers

1002. False

1003. a

1004. Ensign Charles Parker

1005. Sheriff Mort Corey

1006. United Network Command for Law and Enforcement

1007. True

1008. Mike Connors

1009. b

1010. Mr. Beasley

1011. The Ranger

1012. *The Lawrence Welk Show*

QUESTIONS

1013) Madison High School had been converted to a municipal building in the sitcom *Our Miss Brooks*. True or False?

1014) What was the name of Chet Kincaid's mother in the sitcom *The Bill Cosby Show*?

1015) Rod Serling hosted this supernatural series which was one of the original elements in the 1970-1971 NBC series *Four in One*.

1016) What was the name of Julia Baker's uncle in the sitcom *Julia*?

a. Uncle Walter
b. Uncle Ricky
c. Uncle Ed
d. Uncle Lou

1017) Who was the Hoover Bears' star pitcher in the sitcom *The Bad News Bears*?

1018) What was the name of the governor's secretary in the sitcom *The Governor & J.J.*?

1019) What character did George Kennedy portray in the police series *The Blue Knight*?

1020) What was the name of the glass-nosed atomic submarine in the science fiction series *Voyage to the Bottom of the Sea*?

1021) Following Mork's dismissal from the planet Ork, he landed near Seattle, Washington in the sitcom *Mork & Mindy*. True or False?

1022) At what university did Tony Petrocelli attend college in the lawyer series *Petrocelli*?

a. Harvard
b. Yale
c. Princeton
d. Boston

. . . Answers

1013. False, it was demolished to accommodate a highway project

1014. Rose

1015. *Night Gallery*

1016. c

1017. Amanda Whirlitzer

1018. Maggie McLeod

1019. Bumper Morgan

1020. *Seaview*

1021. False, Boulder, Colorado

1022. a

1023) Who was "The Tall Man" in the western with the same name?

1024) Who portrayed Sgt. Charles Wilentz in the police series *Dan August*?

1025) What character did Rose Marie portray in the sitcom *The Dick Van Dyke Show*?

1026) What actress portrayed Joan Stevens in the sitcom *I Married Joan*?

1027) Principal Albert Vane later became the State Superintendent of Schools in the drama series *Mr. Novak*. True or False?

1028) What was the name of Hopalong Cassidy's horse in the western *Hopalong Cassidy*?
    a. Copper   c. Bopper
    b. Topper   d. Hopper

1029) What sitcom spouses lived at 328 Chauncey Street in the Bensonhurst section of Brooklyn?

1030) What actor portrayed Howard Cunningham in the sitcom *Happy Days*?

1031) Who were Karl and Lotte Robinson's two children in the adventure series *Swiss Family Robinson*?

1032) May and Jenny were criminologists in the police series *Hawaii Five-O*. True or False?

1033) Who were the three cops featured in the police series *The Rookies*?

. . . *Answers*

1023. Dep. Sheriff Pat Garrett

1024. Norman Fell

1025. Sally Rogers

1026. Joan Davis

1027. True

1028. b

1029. Ralph and Alice Kramden, *The Honeymooners*

1030. Tom Bosley

1031. Fred and Ernie

1032. False, secretaries

1033. Terry Webster, Willie Gillis, and Mike Danko

QUESTIONS

1034) Nero Wolfe had a special fondness for what type of flower in the detective series *Nero Wolfe*?

    a. carnations   c. violets

    b. roses   d. orchids

1035) What character in the sitcom *Good Times* said: "Make my coffee like I like my men: hot, black, and strong"?

1036) What was the name of Mike Nelson's boat in the adventure series *Sea Hunt*?

1037) Who was the senior editor of *Crime Magazine* in the adventure series *The Name of the Game*?

1038) Susie McNamara of the sitcom *Private Secretary* was always seen in what color?

    a. pink   c. white

    b. blue   d. black

1039) The Space Academy taught its students how to become Solar Guards in the children's series *Tom Corbett, Space Cadet*. True or False?

1040) What was the name of Capt. Amos Burke's chauffeur in the police series *Burke's Law*?

1041) Who did Laura Ingalls marry in the series *Little House on the Prairie*?

1042) Who was the spaceship's pilot in the science fiction series *Lost in Space*?

1043) What was the name of the rabbit mailman in the children's series *Kukla, Fran, & Ollie*?

... *Answers*

1034. d

1035. Willona Woods

1036. *Argonaut*

1037. Dan Farrell

1038. d

1039. True

1040. Henry

1041. Almanzo Wilder

1042. Major Donald West

1043. Fletcher Rabbit

1044) What was the name of the police mechanic in the police series *Chips*?

    a. Harlan   c. Hector
    b. Harvey   d. Hank

1045) "Well, I'll be a dirty bird!" was a familiar expression of this comedian who hosted his own comedy show in the late 1950's.

1046) What actress portrayed Shirley Feeney in the sitcom *Laverne & Shirley*?

1047) Fred was the name of Philip Boynton's frog in the sitcom *Our Miss Brooks*. True or False?

1048) What was the nickname of Bob Collins's secretary in the sitcom *Love That Bob*?

1049) Who was secretary to the two veterinarians in the medical series *Noah's Ark*?

1050) What was the name of the Douglases' chicken in the sitcom *Green Acres*?

    a. Sally   c. Katy
    b. Alice   d. Wendy

1051) Who was WKRP's general manager in the sitcom *WKRP in Cincinnati*?

1052) Tim O'Hara was the only person who knew of the Martian in the sitcom *My Favorite Martian*. True or False?

1053) Who was the uncle and self-proclaimed hotel manager in the sitcom *Petticoat Junction*?

1054) Who murdered Tom Jordache in the mini-series *Rich Man, Poor Man — Book I*?

. . . Answers

1044. a

1045. George Gobel, *The George Gobel Show*

1046. Cindy Williams

1047. False, Mac

1048. Schultzy

1049. Liz Clark

1050. b

1051. Arthur Carlson

1052. True

1053. Uncle Joe

1054. Arthur Falconetti

QUESTIONS

1055) What actor portrayed Mel Warshaw in the sitcom *I'm Dickens — He's Fenster*?

1056) What subject did Robinson Peepers teach at Jefferson High School in the sitcom *Mr. Peepers*?
    a. History   c. Mathematics
    b. Science   d. English

1057) What was the name of Alice Kramden's mother in the sitcom *The Honeymooners*?

1058) Fonzie's "office" was located in the boys' room of Arnold's Drive-In in the sitcom *Happy Days*. True or False?

1059) What was the name of the Bionic Boy in the adventure series *The Six Million Dollar Man*?

1060) What family did Hazel live with on the sitcom *Hazel*?
    a. Bugeys   c. Bridges
    b. Taubs   d. Baxters

1061) What actor portrayed Tod Stiles in the adventure series *Route 66*?

1062) Who were the two radio disc jockeys featured in the sitcom *Good Morning*?

1063) Who was Vernon Albright's boss in the sitcom *My Little Margie*?

1064) Lucy Carmichael was a divorcee in the sitcom *The Lucy Show*. True or False?

1065) Who was the host and narrator of the western *Tombstone Territory*?

. . . Answers

1055. Dave Ketchum

1056. b

1057. Mrs. Gibson

1058. True

1059. Andy Sheffield

1060. d

1061. Martin Miller

1062. Lewis and Clarke

1063. George Honeywell of Honeywell and Todd

1064. False, a widow

1065. Richard Eastham

1066) Which one of the Bradley girls married Steve Elliott in the sitcom *Petticoat Junction*?
   a. Billie Jo
   b. Bobby Jo
   c. Betty Jo

1067) Who were the two young women featured in the sitcom *On Our Own*?

1068) Who was Richard Diamond's police lieutenant friend in the *Richard Diamond, Private Detective* series?

1069) The courtroom series *The Defenders* was aired on NBC. True or False?

1070) What did Randy Stumphill do for a living in the sitcom *Flo*?

1071) What was the name of Frank Faraday's son in the detective series *Faraday and Company*?

1072) What was the name of George "The Kingfish" Stevens's wife in the series *Amos 'n' Andy*?
   a. Beulah
   b. Pearl
   c. Ruby
   d. Sapphire

1073) Who was Margie's romantic interest in the sitcom *My Little Margie*?

1074) How many "stories" were there in the police series *Naked City*?
   a. 5 million
   b. 6 million
   c. 7 million
   d. 8 million

. . . *Answers*

1066. c

1067. Maria Teresa Bonino and Julia Peters

1068. Lieutenant McGough

1069. False, CBS

1070. Mechanic

1071. Steve

1072. d

1073. Freddy Wilson

1074. d

1075) What actor portrayed special agent Jim O'Hara in the police series *O'Hara, U.S. Treasury*?

1076) A daughter was born to Joey and Ellie Barnes in the sitcom *The Joey Bishop Show*. True or False?

1077) What was the name of Tammy Tarleton's houseboat in the sitcom *Tammy*?

1078) Which of the following characters was not a diver in the adventure series *The Aquanauts*?
  a. Drake Andrews
  b. Larry Lahr
  c. Roger Hamilton
  d. Mike Madison

1079) Freddie the Freeloader was pantomimed in the comedy variety series *The Red Skelton Show*. True or False?

1080) What was the name of the Italian Restaurant above which Doris Martin took an apartment during the third season of the sitcom *The Donna Reed Show*?
  a. Palucci's
  b. Amadio's
  c. Donofrio's
  d. Mostardi's

. . . Answers

1075. David Janssen

1076. False, a son

1077. *Ellen B.*

1078. c

1079. True

1080. a